Saving RAINE

Thank You So Much!

This book is a work of fiction. Names, characters, places, and incidents are the product of the author's imagination or used fictitiously. Any resemblance to actual events, locales, or persons, living or dead, is coincidental.

L.B Publishing
3343 Peachtree Rd NE
Ste. 145-712
Atlanta, GA 30326
www.lbpublishingbooks.com

Printed in the United States of America

First Edition: April 2024

For information about special discounts for bulk purchases, please contact L.B Publishing
www.lbpublishingbooks.com

Library of Congress Control Number: 2023920523

Thomas, Marian L.

Saving Raine / Marian L. Thomas - 1st. Ed.

ISBN-978-1-7324880-8-3

Subjects: | BISAC: FICTION / FAMILY LIFE | FICTION / COMING OF AGE | FICTION / CITY LIFE

MARIAN L. THOMAS

Atlanta

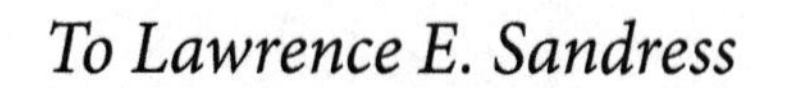

To Lawrence E. Sandress

Acknowledgments

I want to express my heartfelt gratitude to my husband, whose unwavering love and support continually envelop me.

To my mother, your enduring belief in me has been a guiding light. Thank you.

To my dear mother-in-law, your enthusiasm for my writing projects surpasses even my own. Thank you.

To my sister, your excitement, love, and support means the world to me. Thank you.

To my entire family, with a special shout-out to my Uncle Charles Aunt LueAnn, Aunt Sammie, LaShaunè, Keith & Faye. Thank you.

LeAnn Sellers, your unwavering support has been a pillar of strength. Thank you.

To my cherished friends, including Kerry, Mia, Thelma, Beverly, Keasha, K'Asha, Dionne, Kayla, and many others too numerous to name, I extend my heartfelt thanks for being the most enthusiastic cheerleaders on this journey.

And to all my readers, it's your continued support that keeps my passion for writing ablaze. My journey as an author burns brighter because of all of you. Thank you.

"You can't go back and change the beginning,
but you can start where you are and change the ending."

–C.S. Lewis

Prologue

THERE COMES A MOMENT in life when you find yourself standing at a fork in the road, undecided, unsure, knowing you have to make a decision. This way, or that?

The route to the left offers a chance of fleeing from life so fast you can't catch your breath, escaping to an easier place, one in which you can hide away for a time. On your right, you're standing in the middle of the road stripped bare, somehow devoid of feeling and yet ensnared in the worst possible agony, screaming until the tears come cascading down your face.

As my house keys nestle in my sweaty palm, fingers curled way too tight around them, poised outside our five-bedroomed home, I know which road I'm on.

In truth, the moment my swollen eyes shot open this morning, and my head lifted from a tear-soaked pillow, it was apparent.

However, the fact that I slipped on a pair of dark blue jeans that I haven't worn since the day James and I met and a white satin blouse that James loved but I hate because it has a shine to it, confirms that my feet have more than drifted to the right.

But now, as I stand here staring at our fiery red front door, this wretched satin blouse is clinging to my body like Saran Wrap, and I can't determine if it's clinging because this afternoon sun in September has my skin as hot as a cup of freshly made McDonald's coffee or because my body is clinging to a love that has taken up every inch of my heart for the last fifteen years.

Perhaps, it's a little bit of both.

Right now, all I can think about is how I'd give anything for a breeze or something to carry me from here. I pray for anything, anything at all, to rescue me.

In the past, the heady aroma of fall flowers would have filled my lungs sufficiently to alleviate the anxiety occupying this space, but today, not so.

Today, even the violas and pansies that break into bud and bloom around this time of the year seem vacant of any scent, and the more I stand here, the more my mind longs for something to whisk me up into the clouds where I can just float away and pretend like I don't have a care in the world or a broken heart.

At this moment, I'd give anything to be able to look down at my life instead of standing in front of what it used to be.

Trying to breathe.

If anyone were to walk by right now, they would say that I was well put together, only witnessing what's on the surface of my outer appearance, the inner masked so well. They wouldn't look hard enough to see what was brewing inside. And what if they did?

What if they took just a second to step back?

Well, they would see the very sinews and veins of me, no outer skin, no protection, just stark vulnerability, and lungs worn out from screaming.

And if those same onlookers took another second to peer even closer, then, they would see a mad stream of tears only a few split seconds away from breaking free and rushing down the sides of my face.

I take a slow and deliberate deep breath as I slip my house key into the door's lock. It moves with familiarity, bringing back a host of memories better left subdued. The heavy door clicks open, my hand rests on the solid brass handle that James and I had fought over.

"Too old fashioned," he'd said. "The sort of handle an old person would have."

That all changed once Damon, our handyman, installed it.

"Great choice," James then said. "Really suits the door and frame, gives a kind of luxurious feel."

In the end, it became his idea.

How can it be that in everyday life when everything's normal, you don't think twice about the simple stuff like opening a door, or picking out a door handle, until those simple things remind you that another woman placed her hands on them too, acting as if they belonged to her.

As if my James, too, was hers to touch and to kiss and to keep.

The worst part of all of this is that I can't ask James the one question that continues to burn in my heart.

Why?

Chapter One

SOMEONE IS KNOCKING ON the door of my hotel room.

Banging, actually.

My eyes shoot open, my sight resting on the popcorn ceiling directly above my bed. I glance over at the window, expecting to see the sun, but there isn't even a hint of it. It's early. Too early to have someone banging away at the door, making such a horrific noise like that.

I hope they'll realize they're at the wrong door and go away.

Believe me, it happens. It's not the first time.

Even in fancy hotels like this one.

People accidentally knock on your door or try to put their code into your door's security keypad or their key into your reader.

That is a real thing.

Must have experienced it three times this year alone.

Being an author and having to tour twice a year, for three to four months straight, has taught me much about hotel life and the crazy things people do in them.

Like the time when—

My thoughts are interrupted. The hard knock turns into a kick, or maybe it's a fist, causing my bed to shake from the vibrations. Angry as all get out, I tug the covers back, and then sit at the bed's edge, perching precariously before reaching over to turn on the light. As I wipe the sleep from the corners of my eyes and give them a few moments to adjust, the banging intensifies.

My jittery hands set off fumbling at the cell phone on the nightstand, six o'clock appearing on the screen. "Whoever you are that's banging on my door, you'd better have a good reason for this *before the sun can come up* foolishness!" My voice is loud. Even for me, but that's what happens in situations like this.

Anger takes over.

My body shifts, allowing the escape of a slow yawn.

Another kick hits the door.

Please, just stop with the noise!

What to do though?

The person is not backing off, not going away. And just when I'm about to say something I know I shouldn't, my cellphone vibrates, bringing in a text message from Jasmine, my publicist and best friend since kindergarten.

> `Raine, get up and come open the door!`

> `Yes! I'm coming!` I quickly text back.
> `Stop with the banging!`

A few more exclamation marks make their way to the screen, then the phone is allowed to sit back in its nightstand cradle, looking just about as tired and jaded as its owner.

The banging stops, and I slide my feet into a pair of fluffy white hotel slippers.

Groggily, my body somehow manages to slither me all the way to the door, wearing a black satin bonnet over my long and curly, natural brown hair, attired in a pair of black cotton pajamas without which I refuse to ever travel; the bottoms have pockets, you see. I love pockets!

I open the peephole even though it's Jasmine, doing it just to irritate her because let's be real, if she's going to wake me up at this ungodly hour, then why shouldn't she be just as irritated?

My irritation, however, quickly turns into uneasiness. She has not come alone.

Two tall white men are there too, holding police badges, Jasmine standing in front of them, staring back. She appears ashen, unhappy, fractious.

My eyes rest on Jasmine's face.

Are those tears in her eyes?

An uneasiness moves to the pit of my stomach.

I turn the security lock to the open position and slowly open the door.

"Are you Mrs. Raine Reynolds?" one of the police officers asks as he steps in front of Jasmine, who dabs at the corners of her eyes and then glances at my head.

"Yes, that's me," I say, reaching up and quickly removing that black bonnet, stuffing it in the pocket of my pajama pants. "What's this about? Jasmine, what's going on?"

"Chicago P.D. Can we come in?"

"Please tell me what this is about?" I ask again, trying my darndest to keep calm. In my mind, I know it must be something earth-shattering. What else could bring the Chicago Police Department to almost kick my door down, in what feels like the middle of the night?

"Is there somewhere we can sit, Mrs. Reynolds?"

A strange question. What is there in a hotel room—a high-end one at that?

A sofa for four? Yes.

Chaise lounge? Of course.

Their eyes shift toward a velvet gray sofa sitting against a wallcovering that blends perfectly, in light gray and cream hues.

"Tell me what this is about first, please," I say, more forcefully this time.

The tallest officer, the one with a black mole on his chin and a too-short haircut, clears his throat as if he's about to deliver the speech of his life. "Mrs. Reynolds, I'm Officer Sealy O'Connor, and this is my partner, Officer Brandon Brennan. As I said, we're with the Chicago Police Department. Mrs. Reynolds, sorry to tell you, but your husband James Anthony Reynolds was shot and killed in your Atlanta home last night."

My eyes blink rapidly as my right hand moves toward my heart. The police officers step closer as I breathe in so deeply that I'm not far off from passing out.

"What… what did you just say? Shot?"

I know I heard that wrong.

Please tell me that I heard that wrong.

Jasmine rushes over and grabs my arm as my knees begin to shake with sudden fierceness.

Officer O'Connor clears his throat again. "Mrs. Reynolds, your husband…"

The air in the room is sucking the life out of me. Officer O'Connor's lips are moving, but are there any words coming from them?

Something is happening to my heart.

It's not beating.

Chapter Two

"RAINE, I NEED YOU to try and open your eyes," Jasmine says softly to me.

They do open, slowly, and now I am down on the floor in the recovery position, three people staring at my face as if needing to draw a sketch of it later, studying every intricate detail.

The police officers reach down and gently help me to my feet.

No point in asking what happened; I already know the answer to that.

"I'm sorry," I say. "I just can't believe my James is…" My legs wobble again.

"It's a lot to take in," Jasmine says, grabbing a hold of me. "Why don't we get you over to the sofa? Take it slowly, Raine."

My legs begin to move toward the sofa, but a puff of fog has filled my skull. Where my brain used to reside, there's cotton wool or something. A fuzziness. A vagueness.

Some say that in moments like this, they see the life they once had with the person they just lost flash by like a series of photographs. Except I am the one standing behind the camera, snapping away and trying to capture every moment before they fade like photographs always do when time has sucked all the residual life out of them.

As I ease down onto the sofa, the police officers take a seat across from me in matching gray velvet chairs, the ones I photographed yesterday and texted over to James.

> `These would be perfect for my sitting room,` I had texted.

He didn't respond.

Was that when it happened?

Was that when someone snatched away my forever?

I don't bother wiping the wetness from my vision; the police officers' will have seen tears like mine before, many a time. There's nothing to shock them with, everything too familiar.

Even murder.

The way Officer O'Connor produces a few tissues from his right shirt pocket confirms this.

"I'll grab you some water and an aspirin," Jasmine says as my fingertips gently dab my nose.

At the window, a sliver of light traces the outside edge of the curtains. The sun has appeared, which means that a new day has come, and for me, that also means there's no going back to yesterday. A day when everything was apparently all right.

And my James was alive.

"Would you like me to open them?" Officer O'Connor asks, turning to eye the sliver.

I hesitate before saying, "Please."

As the curtains are pulled back, my eyes shut, allowing the sun's warmth to remind me of breathing again. But soon, my attention is drawn back into the moment as Officer O'Connor takes his seat again. He straightens the legs of his pants. As if that matters.

"Here you go." Jasmine walks over to me, handing over a glass of water and an aspirin.

My hands shake so badly I can barely keep the glass up by my lips.

Silence enters the room as the water works its way down my throat. "W-what happened?" I finally ask, placing the glass on the coffee table, Jasmine sitting next to me.

My eyes search the faces of the officers while they each shift in their chairs, shuffling this way and that like young boys asked to sit still while the teacher does roll call.

Officer Brennan sits up in his own seat, pulling out a small notepad, and scouring the pages. "We don't have much for you yet, Mrs. Reynolds. The detective assigned to the case at the Johns Creek Police Department is still trying to put the exact details together."

"But they must know something. You must be able to tell me something."

Are they hiding things from me? Do they think I'm involved somehow? That's how things play out on documentaries. It's always the spouse who did it. Always.

"What aren't you telling me? You can't come here and tell me something like this but then withhold any details." My lips blurt out.

"It's like the officer said, Raine, we have to wait to see what the detective has figured out," Jasmine says in a tone that she often uses with me when she knows I'm upset about something.

I look at her for a second and then move to the edge of the sofa, directing my attention toward Officer Brennan. A deep breath comes, then an exhalation. "I know you're hiding something from me," I say as calmly as I can. "James was my husband. You understand that don't you, Officer Brennan? You must have something for me."

His face shifts some but remains passive. "Yes, ma'am. I understand that. I wish we had more. But until we receive anything, however small, unfortunately, there's not a lot to give and I'd rather not be speculating. I know you also wouldn't want us to speculate. You deserve the truth, and anything less than that will only make things more difficult later."

What's that supposed to mean?

The intensity of my gaze burns into him, wanting him to feel the agony I'm in, wanting him to see it. "Officer Brennan, I have a right to know. I have a right to know what happened to the man that I have loved for fifteen years. Fifteen years, Officer Brennan. If it were you, wouldn't you want to know? Even if the truth hurts. Even if it ripped out what was left inside of you, wouldn't you want to know? Look at me. Do you really think I can hurt any more?"

He leans forward in his chair, the connection our eyes have made remaining unbroken. I fold my hands in my lap, waiting for the answer to my question to drop from his lips.

It's like waiting for water to boil.

Slow and agonizing.

His eyes leave mine, and he begins to scan his notes again. When he looks back up at me, I brace myself and my heart.

"Okay," he says slowly. "At approximately 6:59 yesterday evening, gunshots from inside your Johns Creek home were reported by a neighbor."

"And?" I ask, annoyed with the hesitation that continues to linger in his voice.

Officer Brennan looks over at O'Connor, who nods.

Once again, Brennan clears his throat and allows our eyes to meet.

Jasmine reaches over and places her hand on top of mine.

"After speaking with your neighbors and looking at the evidence thus far, the Johns Creek Police Department believes it's likely that Mr. Reynolds was shot and killed by his…"

"By his what?" I ask, removing my hand. "For goodness' sake, please, just tell me. This stalling is too much. I can't stand all this messing about because anyone can tell there's something you're keeping from me!"

Tiny beads of sweat form around Officer Brennan's temples, but nothing compares to the knots deep within the lining of my stomach.

"Mrs. Reynolds—"

"Oh, please stop with the formalities. I just want this over with."

"It… It appears he was shot and killed by his mistress, ma'am."

My hands grip the edge of the sofa. "That's not possible," I say with absolute faith in my words. "My husband didn't have a… a mistress. He just wouldn't have had one. No way."

"I know this is difficult for you, Mrs. Reynolds."

My anger meets his eyes.

"Oh, so you know?" I lean back into the sofa. "How could you know how difficult this is? How could you even begin to understand? You just told me that my husband of fifteen years has supposedly been having an affair and he's been murdered as a result. How could you understand how I'm feeling after news like that? Explain it to me, because I'm waiting."

"I'm sure he didn't mean it like that," Jasmine says, trying to hold my hand, but my fingers recoil from her touch.

"Shut up, Jasmine!" The words slide off my tongue, followed by instant regret and remorse. There's no way to reel them back in. The hurt look on her face causes me to look away.

Anger and guilt are a terrible mix.

"You're right," Officer O'Connor says as he shuffles forward to the edge of his chair.

I reach down and pick up my glass, wanting to hurl it across the room but taking another sip of water instead. A pointless sip, unnecessary. *Everything* has grown pointless now.

"I'm sorry," I say to Jasmine, placing the glass back down.

"It's okay."

"No, it's not. None of this is okay. How could he do this to me?"

She places her hand on top of mine again. This time, I let her. "They really don't have more, Raine. They're still gathering evidence; isn't that right, Officer Brennan?"

"Yes, that's correct."

Officer O'Connor places a piece of paper on the table. "This is the contact information for the lead detective handling the case. Her name is Tracy Thompson. She's expecting your call. She'll be able to answer any questions and give you the fuller details as they come in."

I look down at the paper as the officers stand up. Jasmine rises too.

"I'll walk the two of you to the door," she says.

"Wait." I take a deep breath and then look up at each of them. "Did they catch her? Did they catch the woman who did this? Who is she?"

Officer O'Connor looks down at me. "Apparently, there was a struggle between your husband and her, and a shot ensued in the process. There were no survivors."

"I see. Was… was that in the house?"

The officers nod, saying nothing.

I look down at the piece of paper again. "I'll go see the detective as soon as I get back into Atlanta this evening."

"We are truly sorry for your loss, Mrs. Reynolds, and I know this isn't the right time to say this, but my wife is a huge fan of your books," Officer Brennan adds, giving me his best shot at a warm smile.

"So was James," I mutter.

Jasmine walks the men to the door.

Chapter Three

TWO HOURS.

That's how long I had aboard the plane to allow the words "your husband was killed by his mistress" to consume my every thought.

How does a person take in words like that, and what do you do with them once you can't bear them any longer?

On the plane, a woman sat next to me. She told me her name, but now I can't remember it. Nor can I recall what she had on, how old she was, or whether her hair was black or brown, but as I stand here at the baggage claim, I remember one thing about her.

What she talked about.

Her children.

I couldn't write a book about her every word, but I do remember how she spoke about them.

With love.

Love.

A word I can't feel right now.

A word that has been replaced in my mind with *mistress, lover, affair.*

And *lies.*

"Excuse me."

I turn around and find a young woman staring at me with a smile that expands her cheeks.

"Are you author Raine Reynolds?"

My head nods, eyes concealed behind dark glasses. Can she see the tears at all?

"Of course, you might not remember this, but last year, you were at a book signing in Little Rock, Arkansas. My sister lives there and I was visiting her."

Just keep smiling, I say to myself as she continues.

"Anyway, the bookstore had run out of your books, so I wasn't able to purchase one that day and have you sign it."

"I'm so sorry about that."

She lets out a giggle. "It's not your fault, Mrs. Reynolds."

In the noisy airport, my gaze darts around, hoping to find anything or anyone that I can use as an excuse to get out of this conversation.

"This is going to sound crazy, but would you mind signing my book? I can't believe I'm actually speaking to you. You're amazing."

Right. Yes. Sure.

I take a quick breath inward and then slowly exhale. "Sure, if you have one on you."

She opens her purse. "I do. I was reading it for the fourth time on the plane. Bought it a couple of weeks ago from this cute little bookshop that also does great coffee." She pulls the book out of her purse. "I'm on my way to see a friend of mine in Florida and thankfully, I had a stopover here in Atlanta." She pauses to catch her breath. "I'm sorry, I know I'm rambling. You didn't ask me why I'm here. It's just… you know, I'm just so excited. I knew it was you."

"I'm happy to sign your book," I say, hoping that will help move this moment along.

"I just love your books."

Oh, for goodness' sake! Just be done with it and go away!

Every part of me wants to scream for her to leave me alone, but I can't do that. She's not the reason for my pain.

James is.

"Do you have a pen?" I ask, almost in a whisper.

Her face lights up, and I yearn for that.

That feeling of happiness.

Of hope.

I fake a smile again, extricating the pen from her tiny, curled fingers with their pretty pink nail polish, so perfect, waiting for her to open the book to the page that she wants me to sign.

Of course, she's going to want some personal message now.

My hands shake while I scribble my name on the designated page without asking for her name so I can write something more bespoke.

I doubt my signature is even legible, but don't look down to confirm this.

No *best wishes*, no *thank you for buying my book!* Just an illegible scrawl.

"Thank you," she says as she closes the book with a disappointed sigh, then places it back into her purse. It makes me feel mean and ungrateful. People like her are my life.

I want to apologize and offer to send her a new book with a more personalized signature, but there it is, my suitcase being tossed onto the conveyor belt.

"I'm sorry," I say, grateful for the interruption. "I think that's my luggage."

Her eyes follow mine. The vast lump of a black suitcase with a purple polka dot scarf attached to it moves in front of us.

"I do that too, only I use a pink scarf," she says, pointing to my purple one.

"Too bad I didn't have pink," I say, even though I've never owned a pink scarf.

I hate pink.

"It makes it so much easier to notice on the carousel," she rambles on. "Many times, I've seen people remove the case, realize it's not theirs and struggle to get it back onto the belt. Kind of embarrassing. Even worse, some get home and find—"

"Yes. They have someone else's baggage!" I enthuse. Fake, of course.

I beam a smile. False too.

Her happy demeanor and energy return at my willingness to engage with her, but the inside of me is only jealousy at what she owns.

Normality. Hope. Joy.

Things I will never feel again.

Chapter Four

THANKS TO JASMINE AND the private car she arranged for me, ninety minutes after walking out of Hartfield-Jackson Airport into the June evening air, I find myself at the Johns Creek Police Department, being escorted into a large room with stark white walls, four very uncomfortable black chairs with a glass coffee table between them, and a non-functioning plastic wall clock.

"Detective Thompson will be in to speak with you in a few minutes," a very young police officer says to me, then rushes out of the room before I can say anything or pose questions.

Seated in one of the black chairs, my body sinks down, eyes closing.

Yet those abysmal palpitations keep coming again, my heart beating rapidly as the urge to get up from my chair and run out of this stark white room tempts me.

A few minutes pass, and then the door swings wide.

Detective Tracy Thompson bearing naturally curly hair like mine, and skin that reminds me of a Hershey's milk chocolate bar, joins me, dressed casually, wearing a nice but simple black pants suit with a cream blouse.

She has a cup of coffee in her left hand and a small notepad in her right.

"This coffee is for you," she says as she eases down into the chair across from me. "You take it black, right?"

"How do you know that?" I ask, reaching out and taking the cup from her.

"I didn't see any coffee creamer in your kitchen cabinet when we were there," she says as she places the notepad on the glass coffee table between us. "No milk in the fridge. Kind of indicative!" She chuckles.

Emotion builds up inside of me at just the thought of police officers rummaging through my life. Our life. Everything that has something to say about who James and I were, or about the life we shared together for fifteen years.

"You probably noticed that we were out of toilet paper as well," I say sarcastically as I shift in my chair and hold the tears back.

She stares at me for a second, blinking once or twice.

Is this some type of game to her?

"I'm sorry, Mrs. Reynolds, I didn't mean that in the way it came out. When I have a case like this, I try to look for things like that, so that when I meet the spouse, I can offer them something personal. I find that a simple gesture like understanding how they take their coffee helps them feel a little less…"

"Emotional," I say.

"Uncomfortable," she emphasizes, then leans back in her chair with the notepad still sitting in her lap. Unopened.

I take a sip of my coffee. As it coats the back of my throat, I silently admit that she's right. The black coffee, just the way I like it, does make my shoulders ease from their tense state, if only for a few minutes. "I'm sorry. I shouldn't have taken it that way. It's been a long day," I say as I place my cup down on the table. "So much to take in."

"I can't imagine what you're going through, but I am sorry for your loss."

The word 'loss' digs into me like a dagger, staring at the wall behind her.

I see James's face and feel nothing but anger.

I'm angry that I have to be here, at a police station.

And of course, I'm angry because of the *reason* I'm here at one.

Tracy reaches down and opens the notepad. She tears a piece out of it and hands it to me. "It's Kleenex. I know it looks like a notepad. My nephew bought it for me."

I smile through the tears. "That's clever," I manage to say.

"It is," she says as she closes the pad back.

I take a deep breath and then place my hands in my lap, gripping the piece of Kleenex like it's the last piece on earth.

"When will I be able to bury my husband?"

"You'll be given possession in about forty-eight hours since no autopsy needs to be completed."

"I want to know her name. Who she was."

Tracy leans forward in her chair a little. "I assumed you would."

She tears off another piece of Kleenex from her make-believe notepad and hands it to me.

"I know I look a hot mess right now."

"If you didn't, Mrs. Reynolds, I might believe you weren't as upset about this as you should be."

"I'm more than upset."

"You have every right to be," she says as she places the Kleenex on the glass table between us, then reaches in her pocket for something. "When you're ready," she says, handing a business card to me.

I look down at it. "I'm going to need more than a shrink to help me get through this."

"I'm sure that's true but calling the number on this card is a good place to start."

"I'll think about it." I take the card, slipping it into my purse.

Tracy leans back and crosses her legs, the expression on her face is sincere but serious if that makes sense.

"Her name was Monica Jefferson," she utters quietly.

I nod. *Monica Jefferson.*

The name plays in my mind like a broken record as I try to remember if James ever mentioned her. "The name doesn't sound familiar. She must have been new," I say.

"She was an attorney working for a different law firm. I think the real question you want to know the answer to is how long the two of them had been having an affair."

I stare straight at her.

Yes, that's what I want to know. You're a woman, wouldn't you want to know how long your husband had been lying to you? But I don't ask or say any of that, just answering with, "You're right. I know it shouldn't matter now, but yes, I do want to know. I *need* to know."

"Based on what we've obtained thus far, it appears everything started about two years ago."

"Two years ago," I whisper, dabbing again with the Kleenex. "Two years."

Tracy tears out another piece and hands it to me. Soon, she won't have any left.

"Thank you," I say after a few moments of silence. "Your nephew's probably going to have to buy you another one of those tissue pad things after we're done with this conversation."

She smiles, but I can tell that there's more to say, words teetering on her tongue.

I stand up and walk over to a small trash can. "Did your nephew really buy that or is it another of your ways to help the spouse feel less *uncomfortable*?" I dump the used Kleenex inside the trash can.

A slow smile spreads across her face. "My nephew bought me the first one, but after I saw how effective they could be in situations like this, I ordered a whole case."

"Very effective." I move back to my seat.

"Mrs. Reynolds, did you ever suspect he was having an affair?"

I reach down and pick up my coffee cup, knowing the drink inside is cold, but it gives me time. Time to allow her rather pointed question to linger in the air for a second. Time to collect my thoughts. "No," I finally say. "Never suspected that he was having an affair. James was made a nonequity partner five years ago at Baker, Henson, and Brown, and being the only black partner, he felt he had to work even harder than the firm's non-black ones. I still can't imagine how he had time to have an affair."

"How were things between you and Mr. Reynolds?" she asks, uncrossing her legs and sitting up straight in her chair. "In general? How was married life?"

My torso shifts, matching her posture. Mirroring it.

"Even if things had been rough between us, which they weren't by the way, it wouldn't have been an excuse for him to go playing around outside our marriage."

I pause for a second, and as I stare again at the wall behind Tracy, James's face is staring back. "Tracy," I say slowly. "There wasn't a fiber in my being that didn't love my husband, and frankly, I always thought he felt the same way, that he loved me and loved the way we were in our marriage.

"I mean if he loved me, I wouldn't be here and having this talk with you, right? I wouldn't have had two police officers coming to my hotel room at six a.m."

"Perhaps," she says.

"There is no 'perhaps' in this for me. If he loved me, there'd have never been a Monica Jefferson, or at least, her name wouldn't have any meaning in my life. If he loved me, I would still be on my book tour right now, and James would still be alive and waiting for me to come home. He would have replied to my message saying how much he liked the color of the chairs.

"He'd have my favorite glass of red wine poured, and we'd be sitting at the kitchen table laughing about something a crazy fan had said or done. Now, the name Monica Jefferson will be with me for the rest of my life. Her name won't just be in my mind; it will dwell in my gut."

Tracy tears a couple more pieces of Kleenex out.

"Mrs. Reynolds, I'm going to say something to you that may sound harsh."

I allow my eyes to meet hers.

"Take from it what you will, but one thing I've learned is that affairs have less to do with love and more to do with selfishness."

"Maybe," I say. "But, at this point, I just want to know why? Why she killed my husband?"

Tracy leans forward.

"Because of the baby. She was expecting."

Chapter Five

I FEEL AS THOUGH I've been driving for hours since leaving the Johns Creek Police Department with a hole where my heart should be, and when the welcome sign for Macon, Georgia, comes into view, I know it's been at least two. Making my way off 1-75, I get caught at a red light with an older woman in the lane next to me. Her dog, which appears to be almost the size of a small horse, is halfway out her car's back window, waiting for the vehicle to move so he can feel a nighttime breeze race through his fur again. The woman glances over at me and smiles.

The dog lets out a bark, and I'm thankful for the light turning green so I don't have to return her act of kindness.

I don't want kindness right now.

What I want more than anything is to have my husband back.

Laughs, touches, and moments that James and I shared consume me, and after four, maybe five miles of crying, an empty mall parking lot beckons. As if driving itself, the car veers off, heading into it.

Just breathe, Raine. Breathe. A small step at a time. Don't put pressure on yourself.

As I roll down my window, the nighttime breeze for which the dog was looking earlier catches a few of my tears.

Leaning my head back, my gaze catches an empty paper bag blowing around the parking lot. Then something else: a couple leaning up against a car, staring into each other's eyes as though love will solve all their problems. Seeing the two of them hurts because I was once that naïve. *Yes, I was like you,* I think. *Naïve and stupid.*

Just wait and see! the hurt in me rages.

My phone vibrates, and when I touch the screen to reject Jasmine's call, a picture appears.

Only, it's not a picture of James and me.

In my mind, Monica Jefferson—or at least how I imagine she looks—is holding a baby. His skin is a rich mocha brown, his eyes round, and his jet-black hair thick and curly like James's when he was a baby. The three of them look like the perfect family, as if I never existed.

Stop it!

I throw my phone in my purse, squeezing my eyes shut so hard, it hurts.

Anything to get that picture out of my mind.

But nothing seems to stop me from screaming.

I scream until the hurt reaches every inch of the car in which I sit, until my throat burns, and the mourning inside me feels as though it's going to burst through the confines of my blouse.

Reaching into my purse, I pull my phone out again, erasing every picture that I can find of James and me, not even thinking about it, just pressing delete, delete, delete.

I delete them all, except one.

The one that has been a part of my life since 1997.

Men in Black came out that year, and Jasmine and I couldn't wait to get our hands on the soundtrack because it featured a song by Destiny's Child.

And this was the year my father's favorite actor, Cuba Gooding Jr., won an Oscar.

Also the year in which James and I stood in front of a Waffle House, waiting for Jasmine to snap a picture of us with her newly purchased camera. The moment she told us to smile was the moment that I felt the warmth of James's hand on the small of my back.

Remembering that moment over the years always brought a smile to my face.

But the moment that sits in my heart came just a few minutes later that day, the one when James whispered in my ear, "I've never met a black woman with eyes so blue. I feel like I'm floating in the deepest blue sky when I look into them."

I never told him, but his words slid down my bones and made a home.

Chapter Six

JASMINE'S NAME DISPLAYS ON my phone screen as it vibrates; if I don't answer this time, she'll call back until I do. She's so annoying like that!

"Hey," I say, placing the phone on speaker.

"I won't ask how you're doing. The cracking in your voice tells me that you're a mess right now. I wish there were something I could do, Raine, I really do."

Outside of the window, there's nothing but stars in the sky. "It's so peaceful up there. Away from all this."

"Up where?"

"In the sky. It's the deepest blue I've ever seen."

"Don't do this to yourself, Raine."

"Do what? Remember? All I have now are memories. To be honest, just before you called, I was staring at that picture you took of James and me outside the Waffle House.

"We'd never have gone there if you hadn't gotten hungry and insisted on a plate of hashbrowns that were scattered, smothered, and covered," I say, running my fingers along James's face, remembering it was only a few days ago I'd used the same fingers to do the exact same thing, only James had been standing in front of me at the time. It's still unreal, unimaginable that he was right here and now he's gone, stolen in the blink of an eye.

I had just given him a kiss goodbye.

"I wish I could take you to the airport this morning," he said.

"I wish you could just go to Chicago with me," I said, placing the suitcase on our kitchen floor. He pulled my purple polka dot scarf out of his pants pocket and tied it around the handle.

"Thanks, I forgot to do that. What would I do without you?" I asked jokingly.

"Thankfully—or worst—you'll never be without me," he said, pulling me to him, wrapping his arms around my waist as if we'd just started dating. I reached out and touched the side of his face with my fingers, feeling the stubble of new hairs trying to come to life on his skin. "Aren't you meeting a client this morning?"

"Is that your way of telling me that I need to shave?"

I smiled.

"Raine, you still there?" Jasmine asks.

"Yes," I whisper. "Still here, in body if not in spirit. Forty years or forever, that's what James said to me that day at the Waffle House after he'd swiped a handful of my French fries."

"I remember that. You two fought for what seemed like hours over that."

"We did. Because it's rude to steal food from a plate. You said that we were fighting like an old married couple. That's when he asked me how long I thought we'd be married, and I said forty years. And *he* said that he could live with forty years or forever."

"I remember hearing him say it. Very sweet. I also remember your father's bright red Cadillac. And I still can't believe he let us borrow it that day to go to Orlando!"

I lean my head back against the car seat, giving a short giggle before reality bites again.

"He loved that car," I say. "I'm sure he only let us borrow it because we'd just graduated from college, and he finally believed I was grown up enough to drive that beast."

Jasmine laughs loudly. "That car certainly guzzled gas like a beast, that's for sure. That's the real reason why I wanted to go to the Waffle House. If I was going to see my boy Mickey, I couldn't afford to eat anywhere else."

"We were both broke. Why we even decided to go to Orlando back then is beyond me."

"Thank goodness you made James pay for our food."

We giggled.

"It was only right because James kept bragging about how he'd just passed the bar exam and was off to become a big-shot attorney."

"What's funny is that Mr. Big Shot just barely paid for our meals, and we only had hashbrowns and French fries. Didn't even have drinks. Just water. I thought we were all going to have to wash dishes!"

"I did too!"

"I wonder whatever happened to that guy he was with, Donovan something or other, I think. He was super cute, and in my opinion, he was a better catch than James."

"You should have gone after him then. He looked like he was a couple of years older, and back then, you were all about the older guys, weren't you?"

"Don't hate just because I had mature taste. Plus, that guy had his eyes on your dazzlingly light skin, and I was too fine to take your seconds."

The laughter emanating from my lips is welcoming.

"So, are you there now?" she asks. "You're parked up, are you?"

She knows me so well, knowing I'd never speak on the phone while driving.

"The Waffle House? No, about a mile from it, in fact. I pulled into a shopping mall to try and catch my breath."

"What? You've been sitting in a mall this whole time?"

"No. In a parking lot. There's a difference."

She heaved a sigh.

"Oh Raine… it's almost midnight. I'll find you a nice hotel and book you a room."

"Book it for a couple of days," I say.

"If you want to stay for a couple of days, maybe I can find you one of those Airbnb's."

"That would be better."

"Then I'll head that way in the morning."

"I can't ask you to do that." I stare back up into the sky, telling myself to be strong.

"Of course, I can. I'm your best friend, and you're not asking me to come, I'm telling you that I *am* coming. There's a world of difference."

"You were always Ms. Bossy."

"That's why I'm your publicist. Give me a few minutes to get things set up. I'll text you and give you the details once I'm done."

"I can't believe he's gone," I say, choked up, hating myself for crying so much. "And don't tell me that I'll get through this. Because I know I will but it's just—it's too much."

After a short pause, she says, "You won't get over it today, of course, but in time, the pain won't hurt as much. Just remember I'm here for you."

"It's not just the pain that needs to go away. It's also the hatred in me."

Chapter Seven

THE SUN HITS ME on my left cheek as I turn over, placing my hand on top of the empty pillow next to me. *Is this going to be my life now? Will the pillow next to me always be empty?*

Sitting up, the rather bold floral wallpaper that covers the walls of the room is suddenly overwhelming. I know the answer to those questions isn't going to suddenly appear between the gold and yellow flowers staring back at me.

Of course, it would be great if that did happen, but just taking in the room and its furnishings pulls me out of my thoughts and helps me focus on something beautiful.

Last night, my tired and swollen eyes barely noticed the sculpted legs of the wing chair in the corner or the elegantly carved dresser with its gold feathers as drawer pulls.

The rich mahogany wood that touches each piece of furniture reminds me of the time James and I were looking for a canopy bed for our guest bedroom. It had to be made of mahogany, he insisted after watching one of those home décor shows. It took us three whole months to find a bed suitable, so he was banned from watching those programs after that.

My eyes travel up the posts of the canopy bed, tracing its intricate carvings with the tip of my finger, unable to help thinking about how much James would have loved not only the bed but also the entire room. Just as my eyes threaten to weep yet again, Jasmine opens my bedroom door and walks in, carrying a cup of coffee and a plate with a bagel on it.

I'd love to look like she does at seven in the morning, especially these last few days.

Her naturally straight black hair is perfectly pinned up in a bun, while her olive-toned complexion looks as if someone airbrushed it. But unlike me, Jasmine never seems to need makeup. She never wears it, and I doubt she even knows how to put it on.

We're both tall and slender, but Jasmine is about an inch taller than I am, still loving to wear extremely high heels, even at five-feet-eight inches. If a man can't deal with it, that's his problem, a good indication that he's not the one for her.

"Take me as I am" or "keep it moving" are her mottos in life.

"I see I came just in time," she says as she hands me the coffee and the plated bagel, and then takes a seat on the edge of the bed. "Let's go for a walk in an hour or so. Shall we?"

"I must look in dire need of some fresh air," I say after placing the coffee and the bagel on the nightstand next to me.

"You look like the air needs you."

"Why does the air need me though?"

"You know how the air is," she says, "always looking for any reason to carry away someone's bad day."

We both smile, and for a second, it feels like one of those moments we used to have whenever one of us got our hearts broken after we thought the boy we had a crush on was "the one." It happened so many times to us both.

I pick up my bagel and take a bite from it as Jasmine checks out my room.

"This room's so beautiful," she says, running her hand over the plush comforter. "My room's similar, but the wallpaper's not as bold as it is here, thankfully."

"I kinda like it," I say, taking a few sips of my coffee. "Thanks for breakfast, by the way. *That's* why I love you—because you feed me."

She smiles again, chuckling, then falls pensive. It's clear she's trying to see if I want to talk about everything Detective Thompson told me.

"I think you're right," I finally say after the silence has lingered around us long enough. "I need the help of the air this morning. To be totally honest, I need everything it's got."

She stands up and places her hands on her hips. "Well then, let's go get you some air."

My eyes take in the room again. "I remember the first time James and I stayed in an Airbnb."

She plops back down on the bed. "I booked that one, didn't I?"

"You did indeed." My head nods. "My first book had just been published, and you'd arranged for James and me to stay at this small Airbnb in South Carolina. I was on my first book tour and the town was so small, that place was the only thing available. It was so quaint. I barely sold twenty copies of my book, but to James, you'd think I'd sold a million."

"Well, he was right, in a sense. That book went on to sell that many copies."

I smile. "If it hadn't been for James, I never would've started writing. He was the one who convinced me to quit my job by the time my second book came out."

"And I tried to get you to quit it even after your first book. Do you remember?"

"I wasn't ready. It was a huge step."

"You were ready, you were just unsure of yourself. Now look at you."

"Yeah, now look at me. But I'd take a successful marriage over a million women's fiction books being sold any day."

"Stop that! Raine, you're blaming yourself for what he did. Please stop. It's so hard to hear."

"I know I am, and I shouldn't, but it's so hard to wrap my head around all of this. The whole thing."

Jasmine reaches into her pocket and pulls out a few sheets of Kleenex.

"I figured you might need these."

"I'll probably need a case of them and a bottle of something stronger than coffee before this day is over," I say, taking the Kleenex.

"There's a store not far from here," she says, "why don't we go and grab you some more of those."

"And chocolate," I say with a wry smile.

"Of course," she says. "We'll get that too."

Chapter Eight

JUST AS JASMINE PARKS the car near the front door of a small grocery store, a group of women come out. Their faces are filled with excitement and laughter. Bags of groceries in their hands. They, I'm sure are buying wine and snacks to prepare for a night of fun later. We too, are here to buy the same, but tonight our faces will be void of excitement and laughter, and our bag will include a few boxes of Kleenex. "I'll run inside," Jasmine says as she follows my stare. "You come in when you're ready, okay?" I nod slowly as she steps out of the car, closing the car door, but my attention remains held captive by the woman wearing a white T-shirt with the words "I Said Yes" on the front of it. Almost immediately, the memory of the day James proposed comes to mind.

It was on a Tuesday.

"Hey," I said to him that evening, "if you're going to be here every day, you better pay rent."

"I'll bring my things over after Friday," James had nonchalantly remarked, lounging on my couch as was his post-work routine. He worked at a small law firm back then.

"Friday? What's happening on Friday?" I inquired.

"We're heading down to the courthouse," he replied, his tone carrying a sense of anticipation.

"For what?" I pressed, genuinely puzzled.

"So I can do more than just sit on your couch, watch television, and then leave," he answered, his eyes twinkling with mischief.

"Oh, so you're ready to stay the night?" I teased, concealing my own eagerness.

"It's been a year. Of course, I'm ready," he asserted.

"Very presumptuous, but I'll allow it," I acquiesced. "What time are we going?"

"I scheduled the ceremony for ten o'clock," he disclosed.

"Why so early?" I inquired, genuinely curious.

"Because then, we'll have the rest of the day," James responded, casting a meaningful look that set my heart racing.

"Well," I stammered, my cheeks flush with warmth, "I'll need to see if I can get the day off."

"I already took care of that," James then said as he got up from the couch, walked his tall, mocha-chocolate self over to me and got down on one knee. "Raine Rene Johnson, if you love me, you'll give me forty years and forever."

My eyes had rested on the burgundy velvet box he held out to me, while my heart took in the love on his face.

"Are you sure you're not just asking me to marry you so you can get in my bed?" I'd asked jokingly as tears flowed copiously.

"I certainly am," James said with a sly smile. "Why else?"

"Then, my answer is yes."

True to his word, James and I stood in front of a judge with his parents and my father present that Friday. My father cried because I was wearing the dress my mother had left for me.

My mother had died four years before then, from cancer.

It was a gorgeous crepe-back satin, strapless dress with a lace-trimmed V-neckline front. How to describe it…? Let's just say it hugged me like it was my mother wrapping her arms around me. I tried not to cry like my dad did, but when I thought about her, the only thing that pushed back the tears was remembering that I was saying *forever* to a man who actually made me want one with him. Oh, and James and I didn't leave the apartment until Monday morning.

Chapter Nine

THE FIRST 1,825 DAYS of our marriage—yes, I counted every single day—came with storms and a rainbow or two. Anyway, we never saw the next thing coming. Six months after we were married, something awful happened. Really, really awful.

James's parents were killed in a car accident on the way to California for vacation. It was the first time I'd seen James cry. The second time came two years later, and that was the night I told him I was pregnant. What a time that was.

We had just traded in my old one-bedroom apartment in Norcross for a lease on a twelve-hundred-square-foot condo in Buckhead. We were like the Jeffersons, James said, but I reminded him that while we were moving up in square footage, we still had only one bedroom!

It was the view of Buckhead that the condo offered up that got us, along with the huge bay windows in the bedroom, the beautiful blue Mexican-style tile floors throughout, and the massive brick fireplace in the front room.

James loved that it was close to the law firm he'd landed at by then—that was Hambrick, Cole, and Donovan. *I* loved that it was just around the corner from a ton of restaurants! Anyone who knows me knows how much I love takeout. My motto is don't waste time cooking when you can just go next door, more or less, for takeout.

Anyway, it was July, and really hot, so hot that the summer heat was causing the Georgia red clay to harden. I'd already started to suspect that I might be pregnant. Every morning, more nausea and a dash for the bathroom.

And talk about tiredness… well, *tired* just doesn't begin to describe it. Most days, I was so exhausted that I could barely get my ad campaigns written without wanting desperately to leave work and go home to nap. Fell asleep in my office chair more than a handful of times.

When I couldn't get my favorite pair of black pants past my hips one morning, it was time to head to the drugstore, and less than five minutes later, my suspicions were confirmed. I was scared to tell James. Children had never been something either of us talked about.

We were career-first people. So anyway, that night, I'd set the kitchen table with candles and his favorite meal, chicken Alfredo. When James walked in at six-thirty, I'd almost lost the courage that I'd been mustering up since the stick in the bathroom trash had turned pink.

"How was work?' I asked him after we'd begun to eat dinner. James put his fork down on the table and looked over at me. He was a lawyer. He knew!

"What is it? What's wrong?' he asked. I put my fork down as well.

"Why do you have to think something's wrong?' I asked.

"Because I know you don't care for chicken Alfredo, and you only get it when you need to tell me something that you think I'm going to be upset about. So come on, out with it."

"Oh, come on, that's not true."

"Raine, really?" he said.

"Yes, really. Just not true."

"Then let me remind you that the last time we had chicken Alfredo, it was because you didn't want to tell me that you forgot to pay the water bill, so our water was going to get cut off. Prior to that, we had chicken Alfredo when you didn't want to tell me that you couldn't go to a client appreciation dinner my firm was throwing because you were up against a deadline for some ad campaign. Shall I continue? Want to hear about two more Alfredo occasions?"

"Okay, maybe, you're right. Just a little bit! And no, you've said enough." I tried to hide that I was smiling, biting on my lower lip, no doubt red from top to toe.

"So, did you forget to pay the electric bill? Is that why we're having a candlelit dinner?"

That made me laugh and gave me the courage I so desperately needed at that moment. "No, I didn't forget to pay the electric bill," I then said, pausing for a second to clear my throat. "But we, umm, we *are* having a baby."

The silence that entered our kitchen was overwhelming. After what seemed like hours, James stood and then walked over to me. He grabbed a hold of my hand and pulled me up and out of my chair. I know it sounds like a scene from one of my favorite Hallmark movies, but honestly, his eyes looked deep into mine and he put his arms around my waist, really tight. His arms rested on my hips, and that's when I saw he was actually crying! Yep, James crying. *Second* time.

Chapter Ten

"YOU SCARED?" HE ASKED as we lay in our bed staring at the ceiling as though we could see our future in the lines of the sky-blue paint.

"About being a mom? Yes. About being a *good* mom? Even more! And what about you, Daddy-to-be? How are *you* feeling?"

James turned over on his side and touched the side of my cheek. The warmth of his fingers comforted me.

"About being a good father, of course. I'd be a fool if I said I wasn't scared by that, wasn't intimidated by that. I think that every man's scared about having his first child if only they'd be honest with themselves. But not for a minute am I scared about you not being a good mom. You've been an amazing wife. A best friend. A lover. A companion. Everything, babes.

"You know, I knew that I was going to marry you the moment you walked into the Waffle House that day. I'd told my friend Donovan, 'Look at my pretty wife who's just walked in. She's fine and smart, that one, and I swear I'll put a ring on her finger!

Well, I will if she'll have me.' Of course he just laughed and said, 'Sure, man, whatever.'"

I turned over toward him and allowed our eyes to meet.

"Right. And exactly how did you know I was smart?"

"Ah, well, you still had your Honor student cords on."

"That's right. And you were wearing a white shirt and a snazzy pair of black dress pants. You were already dressing like a stiff old lawyer."

"My mother always taught me to dress for what I wanted to become. So, blame Mom."

"You wanted to be stiff and old?"

"You got me there. No, I'd wanted to be an attorney for a long time."

He grew serious. Being a lawyer meant a lot to him and his parents.

I placed my hand on his cheek, allowing the warmth of his skin to ease the fears inside of me. "Your deep hazel-brown eyes were so full of life, just like they are now," I said. "And your hair was cut low and neat. You had that same little part in it, like you do now."

He reached over, pulling my body close to his.

"I know that being parents right now isn't how we were going to do this, but I want you to know that I have no regrets. Not a single one. Never."

"No regrets for callously knocking me up," I said playfully, turning over and looked up toward the ceiling. I swear I could see us. I could see James looking down into a crib; we had the biggest smiles on our faces. The happiness on James's expression was so real.

As I turned back toward him, his smile filled one corner of his face to the other. I prayed that we'd really have that moment. That happiness would overtake us, just as I foresaw.

"I hope she looks like you," he said, gently placing his hand on my stomach, closing his eyes.

"It might be a boy though," I said, always playing at being the argumentative wife.

"Well, it might be a girl! No, it's *going to be* a girl. You're too beautiful for it not to be."

He maneuvered his body so he could brush his lips against mine. "I love you, Raine."

I then reached out and pulled him so close, his cologne soaked into my skin.

Chapter Eleven

A FEW LATE FEBRUARY snow flurries could be seen on the tops of every roof from the huge bay windows in our bedroom. I was going into my ninth month of pregnancy. The doctor had put me on bed rest due to a few pains I had been experiencing.

I'm not sure who was more excited about the baby—James or my father.

Every day, I'd discover some new toy that James had purchased or a baseball outfit from my father. It became like a competition to see who could buy the better gift! Not that I minded.

My father was a huge Braves fan and once he discovered that we were having a girl instead of the boy he'd been hoping for, he bought as many pink baseball outfits as he could afford.

He was convinced that if we started putting them on the baby early on, it would ensure that we'd at least have a softball player in the family. As if the clothes would seep into her soul.

But I'd hoped she'd become a writer like me. "Ace, number two" was what James said he'd call her. We all had dreams for her. Sasha. That's what we were going to name her. Well, she never got a chance to wear those cutesy pink baseball outfits, did she?

The tragedy happened on a Wednesday.

James had been out of town for work, so my father had taken over our sofa because James didn't like the idea of me being home by myself. Nor did I if the truth be told.

"Daddy, wake up."

My father didn't move as I stood over him, shaking him, trying to get him to open his eyes.

"Daddy, my water broke."

That did the trick. It got him up and at least rubbing at his eyes. "Are you sure?"

"Pretty sure. Well, unless I've wet myself, of course—and I'm pretty sure it's not that. Daddy! There's a whole puddle of water in my bedroom, would you believe? You'd think it had been raining! But honestly, I feel fine, so I'm sure it will all be okay."

"But you aren't due for another week or so."

He rubbed his forehead as if unable to take it all in.

"Tell that to your granddaughter. Now, I'm going to grab my coat so we can head to the hospital. My suitcase is already by the door. We can get it on the way out."

A week premature wasn't that much, so all would be fine. I wasn't that worried, and my father was more panicked than I was.

My father was standing by the door with my suitcase in his hands by the time I returned with my coat. "Looks like we're ready," I said as the pains began to hit me.

"We should call James."

Another contraction had come by then though, and this one caused me to scream. Sure, every woman knows contractions are strong when they finally set in. But call it instinct; somehow, I knew these weren't only that. Something was wrong. I yelled at Dad, "You can call James once we're at the hospital. Let's just get there first!"

If I could have pulled him, hard, I would have done so. But no, I was too busy fending off agony, seeing the worried look on his face as I grabbed my stomach, yelping like a whipped dog.

"It'll be all right, Dad. You'll see. We can do this. We got this."

I still said it because *I* needed it. His face gave away that not a word of it would he believe. My pain was too visceral, my cries raw and searing, so loud and agonized that not even tears would come. So of course, my father drove us like a madman to get us there; even blue lights and sirens wouldn't have moved us faster. He was stunned, almost silent, his hands whitening each time he heard me sobbing or moaning.

"It's all right, honey," he said now and then, but it emerged as whimpers, and his words were breathy, gasping, plainly overawed by the enormity of it all. His face said what if he lost me? What if *I* lost Sasha? What if he lost us both? Too much to contemplate. Too hard.

I shrieked, gripping the head restraint in front, gripped by the worst pain yet. And he turned, trying to see me in the backseat…

Slam!

Less than a mile from the hospital, we were sent reeling, careening head over tail, down an embankment, into something so hard that it flung Daddy high, striking his head on the car roof then flinging him forward onto the steering wheel.

The truck had veered into our lane and hit us head on.

Daddy, being in the front as the driver, had no chance. None at all. I lay in the back, crumpled and even more wracked with pain.

Sasha died an hour after I gave birth to her.

By the time James arrived, the doctor had already given me the news. I would never be able to have children again.

Chapter Twelve

THAT'S WHEN DARKNESS MOVED into the shadow of our life.

I grew distant. From James, from life.

For the longest time, I felt as if I was no longer a woman, no longer deserving to be a wife. It was my fault Dad had crashed. Should have called an ambulance. Daddy was too distraught to drive that day, any fool could see that. Only I didn't, and now I have no father or daughter.

James did everything he could think of to try and help me find my way back to him. To us. He even signed a lease on a new condo so I wouldn't have to look at the walls that would have rocked Sasha to sleep each night in our old place, walls I now loathed to set eyes on.

The pain in my gut and the holes that Daddy and Sasha had left behind in my heart wouldn't allow me to see what I still had. A husband who adored me, loved me. The only time I felt like myself was at work. At work, I didn't have to think about Sasha or Daddy or, ashamedly, James.

So, I took every project my boss gave me, even asking for more. Projects that, in the past, I would never have taken. I'd stay at the office until I was sure James was asleep.

For the longest time, he was not permitted to touch me. I cried every night, forgetting that I had a husband who wanted a clean pair of undies to put on.

Or a wife to hold him and say she loved him more than anything, and that she was sorry for making him feel like he wasn't enough.

I was so far gone that I'd even talked to an attorney about filing for a divorce, but the moment James found out about it, he gave me the talking to that my soul needed, loving me through the pain. "You are allowed to grieve, Raine! You are allowed to scream at the whole godforsaken world about what has happened to Sasha and your dad. But you are not, I emphasize not, allowed to walk away from what we have. Because *we* have not done anything wrong, and you deserve to be loved by me. And God knows, *I* deserve to be allowed to love you."

That talk helped me find peace, helped me learn to be okay with it just being him and I.

By our fifth year, a rainbow was finally starting to appear after the storm.

But like real rainbows, ours came and went in a flash. All fizzled out.

James lost his job, and for four months, he resented that I had gotten a promotion and was the one paying the bills and keeping things afloat.

The tension that crept into our marriage during that time was heinous, unbearable. It didn't go away until James landed a job at Baker, Henson, & Brown, a new law firm quickly making a name for itself. It was nice seeing my husband begin to feel like a man again.

Years six through nine then slid by like butter, our "smooth and sexy years" being what James called them. By then, we had fallen into a rhythm that kept me smiling like a teenager whenever I thought about him.

Chapter Thirteen

AT THE BEGINNING OF our tenth year, my first book had been published, and it was doing great. Jasmine had opened her PR company here in Atlanta and become my publicist, so I had my best friend back. I thought my life couldn't get any better. But against all odds, it did.

James came home around four o'clock on a frosty Wednesday in December of 2008. I was sitting in the second bedroom of our overpriced apartment near Lenox Mall, also dubbed as my home office. My head was down in editing the copy for a new ad that had to be turned in soon.

In less than ten minutes, actually.

"Ace, where are you?" James asked.

"In my office," I shouted back. "I need ten minutes."

"You still haven't turned in the copy for that new ad you're working on?"

"Oh, you know me. I write my best stuff twenty minutes before it's due," I shouted as my fingers continued to type quickly. "It's when I get all my inspiration."

I could hear his footsteps as he walked toward me down our hallway.

"Hold on, I'm writing the last sentence," I said, looking up briefly to find him standing in the doorway with his coat on, looking down at his watch. "Done, and with a second to spare!"

"You remembered to hit the send button?" he asked.

I glanced down at my laptop, quickly back to my email to double-check.

"Yep. It's sent."

"Good. I would hate to have a repeat of what happened to you last week."

"Me too. I thought Kevin was going to fire me. He was so mad."

James walked into the room, but I noticed him glancing down at his watch every few seconds. "Oh, please," he said. "You're Kevin's ace, and he knows it. Besides, you still got that project in, and it was only a few minutes late give or take twenty minutes, once you realized you forgot to hit SEND."

"In the ad business, a few minutes, let alone twenty, means everything when the client's looking for it to air in a day or so." I had turned completely around in my chair so that I could face him fully. "Anyway. What are you doing home so early, and why do you keep looking at your watch?"

The smile that came upon his face filled the whole room.

I admit, I was always a sucker for James's smile. The way his lips would curl up was just so sexy to me, but it also meant he wanted something. "What's up?" I asked.

"What makes you think something is up?"

"Let's see, it's four o'clock in the afternoon, and you're home. You never get home before seven most nights, and you're still wearing your coat with that super-sexy smile of yours plastered on your face."

His smile then went wider.

"Grab your coat?" he said.

"Why, are we going to look at puppies?"

"Why in the world would you think we are going to look at puppies?"

"Umm, maybe because I saw a picture of one on your computer screen the other day."

He stared at me for a moment, serious before his smile returned. "No, we're *not* going to look at puppies; you know we can't handle a puppy with our crazy schedules."

"Our schedules aren't that crazy. Lots of people have worse."

"Let's talk about it another time. Right now, I need you to hurry up," he shouted as he walked out of the room.

I jumped up and rushed into our bedroom to grab my coat from our shared closet, threw my favorite black leather Michael Kors boots on, and then hurried to meet him at the front door.

The moment I reached him, he quickly pulled me into his arms. "I love you," he said as he leaned down and placed his lips on mine. Since James was over six feet tall, I always had to stand on the tips of my toes when we kissed. But I never minded. It was sweet and romantic, like two star-crossed lovers from the 1920s, the small slim female and the taller protective man.

I loved being wrapped up in his arms, feeling the strength of them around me. Feeling the love of his heart on my lips.

He had started to pull away slowly, but I pulled him back to me.

"As much as I welcome that invitation, we have to get going."

"What invitation?" I asked with a sly smile.

"Come on, let's go. We're already going to be stuck in traffic at this time of day," he said.

"You still haven't told me where we're going. You really expect me to just acquiesce and let you drive me anywhere, do you?" I teased. "My mother warned me about men like you!"

"You'll see. It's a surprise that you'll love."

James had been right. The traffic that day had been horrific, and I could see the frustration on his face every time he glanced at the clock in our Lexus RX350.

I was always so nervous in cars when we were in busy traffic, ever since the collision, especially if we were in some kind of a rush. It would remind me of that day and of the mistake I had made, hurrying my dad into our car when there was so much to worry about. I fidgeted with my hands, wringing them, looking outside fretfully as if the roads would swallow us whole.

After thirty extremely long minutes on Lenox Road, James finally had hit Georgia 400 heading south, then 285 East, and by the time we exited off onto 141 going north, I thought I was going to burst from not knowing where we were headed. The anxiety was admittedly easing.

When James drove up to a gated subdivision called John Creek Country Club and gave the uniformed security guard his name as if he was on the guest list or something, my mind went crazy trying to figure out what the surprise was.

"Are we visiting one of your clients?" I asked when we pulled up to an all-brick home with a three-car garage. "You should've told me! I would've worn—"

"Shh," he said. "You're fine. You're always fine."

There was a black Mercedes parked in the driveway.

"Whose car is that?"

James didn't respond, simply pulling the key from the ignition. Then he turned to me with this serious look.

"Five years ago, when I lost my job, I didn't treat you right. You thought I was resentful of your promotion, but in truth, Raine, I was proud of you, not resentful, and I just couldn't show it because I always wanted to be the provider, you see? Having you pay the bills felt like an attack on my manhood, but you never tried to make me feel less of a man. You just stepped in and handled things and never lost confidence in my ability to find something else.

"And in time, quite a long time as things turned out, I did find something. And now, I would like to say thank you for everything you did. And for the woman you are."

I reached to touch his face, allowing my hands to gently stroke the left side of his cheek.

"You don't need to thank me though," I remonstrated. "It's what wives do for husbands."

"Well, you may say that, but many wives wouldn't. I love you so much, Raine."

He then stretched over again, opened the glove compartment, and pulled out a set of keys. "Welcome home." And a tentative, nervously excited smile sparkled in his eyes.

"Are you serious?" My eyes were barely able to pull themselves away from looking at the front of the home. "This house is huge! We… we can't live in this! Y-you! What've you done?"

"Well, admittedly," he began. "It *is* huge. It has five bedrooms and a large bonus room, so now you can have a real office and a workout room. And a room for the puppy we won't be having." He grinned ear to ear, still relishing the joy of teasing me.

I shot him a look with one eyebrow raised.

"I'm not saying that you're fat, Raine," he said, laughing at my facial expression. "You always talked about having a home with a workout room. Well, now you do."

I couldn't help but reach over and hug him. "I can't wait to see inside."

"I can't wait for you to see it, too. The real estate agent's waiting inside." James reached to open his door, but I stopped him.

"Wait, how are we going to afford this? How are we going to buy it?"

"Oh no," he said, eyeing me with a look of eagerness for us to get inside. "We're not going to buy it. I'm sorry if I gave you that impression."

"What?" Now *I* was confused. My face fell and I couldn't hide it.

He couldn't keep me in misery and suspense any longer.

"Look, I was made a nonequity partner. I didn't want to tell you until after I closed on the house. The ink's barely dry on it. So, it's true. We're *not* going to buy it. I already did!"

I thumped him on the arm, playfully. "Oh, *you!* You had my heart sinking... So, it's ours? Really? You're not going to say something else in a minute?"

"It's ours."

I reached over and hugged him again. "Congratulations on making partner! You worked so hard for it, and you deserve it. I'm so proud of you."

The pride that was in his eyes filled my heart and overflowed it. Pride at buying this for me, for us, after so long where he must have worried that he would never get to this point in his life.

"It's not like being an equity partner with voting rights in the firm's affairs or a share in the profits, but I'm the first black partner. I can hire a secretary, but I'm not sure I need one."

"She had better be old or ugly," I said with a chuckle.

"It doesn't matter if she looks like Ms. USA; you will always be the only woman I love, Raine. I will always belong only to you."

"And I will always only belong to you, Mr. Reynolds, non-equity partner at Baker, Henson, and Brown."

"I love the sound of that."

He moved his hand up and gently pulled my face close to his. When his lips met mine, I felt as though his words had engraved themselves into my heart.

Those words were supposed to mean something. "They were supposed to be true," I say to Jasmine as she climbs back into the car after placing a couple of bags in the backseat.

"What words?"

"Sorry, I've been going down memory lane as they say," letting out a heavy sigh. "I'm also sorry that I didn't come in to help."

"No worries. You looked like you needed some time."

"Two years. That's how long the police detective said he'd been seeing Monica Jefferson, a paralegal at his firm. That means that James was planning to leave me."

"You don't know that for sure."

I look over at her. "Yes. Unfortunately, I do."

"How though?"

"They were having a baby."

Stunned, she glances out the window for a second before turning her attention back toward me. "How did you find that out?"

"The detective told me."

"Wow! I'm glad I picked up an extra gallon of chocolate ice cream," Jasmine says, pulling out of the parking spot.

Chapter Fourteen

THE WORLD DOESN'T STOP for anyone's grief, certainly not for mine.

It doesn't stop to catch the tears that you shed or to wipe them away.

The world absorbs them and keeps moving.

As Jasmine and I sit on a bench at the park just around the corner from the B&B, watching people walk, run, and jog past us, I find myself angry at the world for its ability to recover and move on from all the pain, grief, and tears its seen. I'm angry, too, at all the walkers, joggers, and all the people who get to go about their day so carefree.

And right about now, I'll do anything to stop the crying.

I'm sick of it.

"In a way, I guess it's good that Chicago was the last stop on your book tour. By the way, I let your publisher know that you'll be taking a break for a few months. Of course, they offered their condolences and said to take as much time as you need," Jasmine says as we both stare at a duck splashing in the small lake a few feet away, reveling in cleaning its feathers.

I sigh as I look over at her, seeing the concern on her face. We've been friends for a long time, and while the tears that make their way down my face are nothing new to her, they've never been from a situation like this.

"To date, I've written nine books. When my third book came out, James took me to Paris. He said that researching Paris and actually breathing it in were two different things. He was right. In Paris, I felt like I found my being. It felt so right to be there. I hated to come back. To be honest, I just wish I could have stayed. Maybe I should go back there."

"Maybe. In one of your books, you wrote that Paris was the antidote to a heart poisoned against love. Do you think that's you, Raine? Has this poisoned you against love?"

"I don't know. But anyway, I don't even want the antidote for a heart poisoned against love. I need the antidote for tears. Something that will make them stop. I keep making a fool of myself."

"No, you really don't. People come to parks to cry all the time. It's what parks were invented for! Going to Paris isn't going to instantly take the tears away. Only time can do that."

She hands me a few Kleenexes from out of her purse. I wipe my face as we watch a mother duck swim by with her little ones closely behind her.

"I think *that's* why he did it."

"What do you mean?"

"I mean that I think James cheated on me and our marriage because I couldn't have one of those," I say, pointing to the ducklings.

"A duck?"

"You know what I mean."

"James didn't cheat on you because you couldn't have a baby, Raine."

"How do you know?"

Jasmine takes a deep breath, and when she exhales, the familiar touch of anxiety begins tapping me on the shoulders.

"I said that I was going to take it to my grave."

I gasp, though it's silent.

My eyes search her face as the anxiety moves from my shoulders down to my fingers. "Tell me," I say, placing my shaking hands in my lap.

"You ever wonder why I didn't come to your wedding?"

My voice cracks as I respond, "I assumed it was because we didn't plan one. James and I just went down to the courthouse. When I called you to tell you about it, I never exactly expected you to jump on a plane and come to Atlanta that fast. I mean, that'd have been insensitive."

"Raine, of course, I would've wanted to come no matter what. You're my best friend. You know that I would have paid for a plane ticket or driven if I had to, without hesitation. I wouldn't have missed that day. Not a chance. Not for all the tea in China."

I can feel my face shifting as the confusion pushes through me. "So why didn't you?"

She glances at the mama duck and her babies as they make their way over to the other side of the lake.

"Eight months after you and James started dating," she begins, looking just as pained and troubled as I am, "I came back to Atlanta to see my parents for a few days."

"Yes, I know. I remember that. I remember being mad because I was going to be out of town for a company event and wouldn't get a chance to see you."

"Right. Well, I didn't get a chance to see you because of that, but I did see James."

"Where?" There is fear gripping my belly.

"My parents and I had gone downtown for lunch. You know my mother, a sucker for seafood, wanted to eat at this new sushi restaurant. The place was busy when we arrived, so I went in to see how long the wait was and to use the restroom.

"On my way there, I had to do a double take; there was your James, sitting in a booth next to a woman. I was getting myself ready to head over to say hi, thinking she was a client, but then stopped in my tracks. James leaned across the little table, brazen as anything, and kissed her."

"On the cheek…right?"

She looks at my ever-hopeful face, but we both know the answer is obvious.

"No. Not on the cheek," she says anyway.

My mind is in a whirl of turmoil as I struggle to stop myself from vividly imagining the scene.

"He didn't see me," she says, after a moment or two. "And to be honest, after that, I no longer wanted to go to the restroom, so I hauled it out of there as fast as I could and made an excuse to my parents. I can't remember exactly what I said, but it involved work or something."

I place my hands over my mouth to keep all the questions and anger from bursting out.

At her.

And James.

"That evening, I called him and asked if he and I could meet. I told him I had a surprise for you and wanted to leave it with him. We agreed to meet at that coffee shop that used to be around the corner from the apartment you lived at then."

The anxiety that was in my fingers travels onward, down to my toes.

"At first, he tried denying it, but he knew I'd caught him when I was able to describe the woman in detail, even what they both had on. I told him about seeing the kiss and that it looked passionate between them. And yeah, his demeanor changed to one of guilt.

"I never told you because he swore that what I saw was him ending something that he should have put an end to right after you started dating him, when he realized he was in love with you. The passion, he said it was the emotion of the ending of what they'd had. That he just knew they would never see one another again. That he'd hurt her. It made sense and can you believe, I even apologized. I hate myself for that now. I really let you down and I'm sorry."

An uncomfortable silence sits between us, and I know I should say something, but honestly, I can't find the words. Finally, I say, "James was obviously a great liar, but, you should have just told me. I mean, I wish you had."

She nods a couple of times.

"In hindsight, I probably should have told you, yes, but he swore to me that he'd ended it, you know?"

"But you obviously didn't believe him, and that's why you didn't come to the wedding."

"No, it's not quite like that. I didn't come because I knew that if I saw you, I'd feel disloyal and would have told you. Please trust that it took everything I had in me not to tell you. You were so happy when you called to say that you and James were getting married, and honestly, wrecking a relationship—a good one by all accounts and appearances—wasn't something on my list of wishes. I wanted to save you from worrying about a goodbye kiss and a relationship that was now over and done with, so why hurt you with the news of it? Plus, I really thought he loved you, so I took his word, which wasn't my greatest choice and is one I will live to regret. I just wanted to save you from—"

What? Save me? Her words inflame me.

"I didn't need 'saving,' Jasmine! I needed the truth, and you did have almost four months to tell me the truth. Best friends, remember?"

"I've never forgotten that, and I have been that for you as long as we've known each other. But let's be real here, Raine, it wasn't my responsibility to tell you about her; that belonged to James.

"You know, lots of best friends tell the other about their man cheating, and it breaks the friendship. Lots of women in your position don't want to hear it."

I can't say I agree with her and can't say that I disagree. All I know is that I feel betrayed by the two people that I loved the most.

"Did he tell you what her name was? What did she look like?"

"Oh, come on, Raine. It was fifteen years ago. You want me to draw a sketch or something? I can hardly remember what I looked like myself that long ago."

"Stop trying to save me, Jasmine. I know you. It's all over your face."

Our eyes meet. She exhales loudly, lips pressing into a fine line. "Her name was Monica. They went to law school together."

Chapter Fifteen

HERE I AM AGAIN, staring at the floral wallpaper that covers this room, looking for it to tell me how the heck I'm supposed to breathe.

Or to forgive.

Or forget, even in time.

If Jasmine had told me about James, would I have believed her?

As I reach over to turn off the light, my phone rings.

"Mrs. Reynolds, it's Detective Tracy Thompson."

"Hi," I say, hating to hear her voice though I know she's only doing her job.

"I know it's late, but I thought you should know that your home's been released."

I lean back up against the wall of the canopy bed. "I hadn't even thought about that house."

"I'm sure you've got a lot on your mind as you make the preparations for your husband's funeral. But it's just something we have to do once the investigation is complete and forensics have done what they do."

"I'm going to have him..." I can't bring myself to finish the sentence.

"You're going to have your husband cremated. Is that what you were trying to say?"

"Yes. Yes, that's what I was trying to say. It's something James and I talked about when we lost his parents. That's how he wanted me to handle things, and of course, he put it in writing, so I feel compelled to honor his wishes."

Why am I even telling her?

"You're a better woman than me. I doubt that I would even take his wishes into consideration. But that's me and we're all different. Mrs. Reynolds, I really wish you the best and that everything gets resolved for you. You impress me; you're very strong."

I can't help but drop a tear or two as her words sit inside my head and roll around for a second. "I don't know if I'm a 'better woman' than you for considering James's wishes, but he was my husband, and up to the moment I opened my hotel room door to let the police in, I thought I was his loving wife and that nothing could damage the love we had for each other."

I can almost swear that I hear her gulp as if fighting back emotion at my words.

"Anyway," I say, pushing my fingertips through my unkept hair. "I still haven't contacted his office or our personal attorney."

"Give yourself a few more days."

"I just want this to all be over. I honestly feel like I'm losing it."

"I'm sure. For what it's worth, the card that I gave you when you were here, hopefully, you will call the number on it and give it a try. Just try it Mrs. Reynolds, even if it's just once. Most are skeptical at first, and I totally get it, but so many find it beneficial.

Give it time. If I didn't think it would help, then believe me, I would never hand the number out."

"Maybe, but I doubt it will be much help."

"Look, let me be honest here and tell you something hardly anyone knows. The person on that card helped me. In full transparency, he didn't just help me. He saved me. Like you, I was doubtful at first, but people like him are experts at what they do. Really, if it weren't for him—"

"What did he save you from?"

"From leaving life."

"I'm not going to take my own life if that's why you're recommending that I see a shrink."

I hear her sigh.

"He's not a shrink. At least, not in the traditional sense. He's more of a listener, and Mrs. Reynolds, you should know that you don't have to take your own life to leave life."

I hold my cellphone to my ear, not knowing what to say to that. But she's so right.

"Thank you for the call, Detective Thompson," I finally say. "And your words do help."

"Call me Tracy. It will take a few more weeks before we can release your husband's personal belongings, but someone will let you know as soon as they are available. Meanwhile, feel free to go to the house if you wish."

"Thank you, Tracy," I say, then a knock drums against my bedroom door.

Jasmine opens the door slowly. "I saw that your light was still on. Can I come in?"

"I'm surprised you even asked. Don't you normally just barge on in?"

She gives me a half smile as she walks over and stands beside the bed.

"Look, there's no way I can sleep. You're upset with me, and it gets me here."

She thumps her chest, right over the heart.

I struggle to find the right words to say to her and can't stop the anger in my voice from spilling out. "This isn't like you stole my favorite sweater or something, Jasmine, I really feel like you betrayed me."

She takes a seat on the bed.

Her red eyes tell me that she's been crying; Jasmine rarely cries.

"I'm so sorry, Raine."

"Hey, come on… come on." I stroke her back. "I absolutely don't doubt you are sorry, and yes, James should have told me. I'm not going to lie, I'm still mad at you, but time will heal that as well, I'm sure."

"I hope so. I don't want to lose you as my best friend."

"You're not going to lose me," I say as I glance at one of the bed posts and think about James. "I feel like I'm going to owe *time* every dime I have."

"Good thing you're loaded then. I hear it's because of your phenomenal publicist."

I can't help but laugh, loving this woman so much, even now.

Jasmine stretches out at the foot of the bed. "I'm also sorry for stealing your favorite sweater when we were in the sixth grade so I could wear it to the school dance, even though you were planning to wear it too."

I pick up a pillow and hit her softly with it.

She tries to act as though the tap from the pillow hurt, and for a moment, I mean a split-second, it feels like old times.

"You're such a baby," I say.

"You're just jealous because I have baby soft skin."

"Whatever."

We both stare up at the ceiling and enjoy remembering good times.

For me, the sixth grade comes to mind.

And Barbara Franklin.

Barbara was a tall, skinny girl who always wore her hair in two French braids. She had two older sisters who also went to the same school as Jasmine and me.

And just like her older sisters, Barbara was a bully. Every day, she would find some reason to pick a fight with me, and Jasmine was the one to tell my mother about it. And it was Jasmine who also told my teacher. Because of Jasmine, I had a great seventh grade.

She always had my back.

Always saving me from something or someone.

"James wanted to be cremated, so I'm going to honor his wishes," I find myself blurting out.

She sits back up. "Do you want to do a memorial service as well?"

I grab the pillow back again and pull it into my chest like a security blanket. "We knew a lot of people, so I think I should. It would look bad if I didn't. Not that I much care what people think, but you know, for James… he would want me to hold one. I'm sure people know what happened by now, but I think it's best."

"No one knows. Not even the press. I've made sure of that, and I phoned James's office and explained that he had been shot and killed after someone broke into your home. Of course, they were absolutely horrified. They offered their condolences and asked me to keep them informed regarding funeral arrangements."

I stare at the bedposts again. "I know what I'm about to say may sound horrible, but I wish that's what really happened. It would almost make this bearable. Not completely, but almost. Removing the added trauma of him being unfaithful."

"I wish that were the truth too if I'm being honest."

We share a moment of silence.

"I know it shouldn't matter," I say, "but I want to know what she looked like. You didn't say earlier. Was she tall? Slim? Was she really pretty?"

She stares at me with a concerned look on her face. "Why do that to yourself? It's only going to make this hurt more, Raine. Please, it just won't help you."

"I know, but wouldn't you want to know? Wouldn't you want to know about the woman who robbed you of your husband long before she pulled the trigger on him?"

She nods.

"I would, and then I'd probably find out where she lived and burn her house down."

"Yeah, you would," I say with a half-smile, knowing she's serious.

"Where's your phone?" she asks.

"Why?"

"I can tell you what she looked like fifteen years ago or we can Google her and see what she looks like now, or before..." She pauses. "Just give me your phone."

Putting the pillow down, I grab my phone out of my purse.

"You sure you want to do this?" she asks.

"Here," I say, after entering the password.

She looks down at the screen but doesn't say anything when she notices that the photo of James and me isn't there.

"Add that she was an attorney," I say as she pulls up Google. "She didn't work at the same firm as James, but it had to be close."

I watch her fingers move through the web pages that come up, until she stops.

"Last chance," she says.

I take the phone from her and look down at the screen. Staring back at me is not just the woman who killed my husband but also the one who was carrying his child.

Chapter Sixteen

WHEN YOU'RE GOING TO a memorial service, you expect the sky to be dark. You look for rain and the sound of sadness.

As Jasmine and I step into the black sedan that will take us away from the place where an urn sat high on a shelf with the remains of James inside, I look up, seeing nothing but sunshine.

And hear nothing but birds chirping.

And the sky doesn't have a single cloud in it.

Everything is perfect.

Everything except me.

"I wonder how many of James's colleagues knew about the affair. Do you know how many times I visited his office in the last two years? Looking at it now, they must have known."

"Oh, come on, I very much doubt that. I mean, it happens in movies, not real life."

I look over at her.

"It's true. And Raine, you knew seeing the people he worked with would be difficult today."

"Yes, I knew it would be difficult, but whenever someone came over to offer their condolences, I wanted to ask them if they knew.

"I sat there, staring at that urn as people spoke about how much he talked about me at work and how much he loved me, and I wanted to scream at them to stop with the lying. They were only saying those things out of obligation. It's just what people say at funerals. It was all glib and meaningless. And I wished they'd stop."

"I'm sure most of them were sincere."

"I doubt it," I say, glancing out the window, envying the calmness of the women I see as we drive by. Without a doubt, they have worries and some of them have been through Goliath-like trials, but I doubt whether any of them are saying goodbye to a husband shot and killed by a mistress.

Everyone wants to tell you how they understand what you're going through, but how can they? I'm wearing a shoe size in which none of them could walk.

Not even Jasmine.

These last two weeks have been unbearable, but today has passed even beyond unbearable. Today has been nothing but a lie.

James lied to me for two years, and today, at that service, *I* had to lie to everyone too. It's like a vile disease. James was the first to catch the virus of lying, and now he has transmitted it to me.

For sixty long and excruciating minutes today, I've had to pretend that someone broke into my home and shot and killed my husband.

When exactly does the lying stop?

And what about the mistress? Are her people lying about her too?

I can't bring myself to say her name anymore, but her face has been etched into my every thought since I first saw it. I can't sleep at night without seeing it there, her dark brown eyes laughing at me.

She wasn't just an attorney; she was a partner at one of the biggest firms in Atlanta.

And she was beautiful.

A beautiful, proud black woman.

I'm not going to lie; it would have been easier if she had been white like Jasmine or at least younger than us.

But she was none of those things. She had everything going for her, including James.

I drive myself witless staring at her photograph online, hoping to find a flaw. A freckle. Signs of Botox or cosmetic surgery, saggy skin, dry skin, crow's feet. Anything.

But there is nothing—at least not that a photograph can show.

"Can you ask the driver to pull over?" I say to Jasmine as we come to a traffic light.

The moment the car stops, I open my door, jumping out. "I'm sorry, I just need a minute."

I feel as though I'm suffocating, leaning against the side of the sedan.

Jasmine opens the door at her side, getting out. "Of all the days I forget to bring extra Kleenex," she says as she leans up against the car beside me.

"For once, I just want to let the tears run, you know? Does that make the remotest bit of sense? Wiping them away doesn't stop them or the pain from taking over. So why fight it?" I look over at her. "I'm tired of fighting both. It's like trying to mop the kitchen floor when you have a huge dog that just goes outside, rolls in mud, and comes right back in. You just keep on mopping, and there's more mud, and more mud, and more mud… So, I surrender."

"If your mother were here right now, she'd have the perfect words to say to you. Your father would pull you into his arms and let you cry on his shoulder. He wouldn't care that you were soaking his favorite white shirt. I don't have the perfect words or a white shirt to offer you, but you know I've got a shoulder you can cry on. The shoulder that's always been here for you."

I move over and lean my head on her, exactly as she says. "I'm going by the house next week. It's time that I surrender to doing that as well," I whisper.

"When you go, you should know that I called one of those trauma scene cleanup companies to give the place a once-over. They should be about finished. They were able to paint the walls in the living room the same color as before, and they made sure the carpet was replaced where the…"

"The blood was," I say, finishing her sentence.

"Maybe we should talk about this later."

I stand up and finally wipe the tears away. "It's okay, and thank you for taking care of that," I say. "That's something that totally slipped my mind."

A long sigh escapes as a man walks past us and smiles in our direction. "I don't know what I'm going to do with that house. Part of me wants to be bold like you. Burn it down."

She laughs. "I actually thought about doing that for you. Then you wouldn't have to decide what to do with it and you could have the insurance money. But I guess it's too late for that."

"Maybe, but then we'd both be in jail."

"True. And I never did look good in stripes," she says.

I give her arm a pinch. "Stop it…" She's making me giggle.

"It's beautiful," I say as we stare at a mural painted in front of us.

"I always loved the blue butterfly," Jasmine says. "Whoever painted it has a real flare for color and detail."

"James would have hated it though," I say.

"Good, I like it even more now."

"You are a mess."

"My mother reminds me of that every chance she gets. I keep telling her to remember where I got it from. Now, let's get both of our butts back to my place so we can open a bottle of wine. After today, we deserve it."

"Maybe *two* bottles."

Jasmine turns to open the car door. "Works for me," she says, sliding into the seat and moving over toward the window.

"Thank you for letting me crash at your place this long," I say, scooting in next to her and then closing the door.

"Well, you're welcome to stay as long as you want," she says as her phone rings.

From my purse, I pull out a Kleenex, and the card that Tracy gave me falls on the floor.

The name on the card captures my attention as Jasmine answers her phone.

Are you going to save me, Mr. D. Carter?

Chapter Seventeen

JASMINE BELIEVES THAT KNOWING the "why" of things isn't important. To her, it happened and knowing the "why" isn't going to undo that fact. I can't say she's wrong, but for me, not knowing why James did what he did, is killing me.

Maybe, I do need to see a shrink.

Every day since James's memorial service, I've stared at the card that Tracy gave me, even picking up my cellphone a few times to dial the number when the pain became overwhelming, but I couldn't bring myself to make the call.

And last night, after two glasses of wine, and a box of Kleenex, I tore it up and threw it in a trash can.

But now, as I stand in the foyer of our home, smelling all the fresh paint, I desperately wish I still had it.

Walking into the living room, my eyes travel up the wall looking for a sign of what occurred in here. The photos from the police report told me where they found the bullets even though the holes have now been filled in, sanded, and painted over.

Wouldn't it be nice if I could do the same? Fill in the holes of my broken heart and then sand them away as if they never existed?

I move to the carpet, and when I close my eyes and then open them again, I see the outline of where James's body was found. Kneeling, I run my hands over the spot as the tears come.

There's an outline of a body next to his, but I refuse to acknowledge it.

That outline has taken everything away from me.

Jasmine would tell me that "the other woman" couldn't have taken anything from me that James didn't give her, and I suppose there's some truth to that.

Then there's our velvet cream couch. I remember the time that James spilled a glass of red wine on it. It took us an hour to get the stain out, and when we were done, he reached over and poured my glass of wine in the same spot! "What on earth did you do that for?" I asked, my eyes wide, also shaking my head in bewilderment.

"Because I want another hour with you."

We didn't eradicate the second stain that night, and I had to call a cleaner the next day who charged us over a hundred dollars, but James felt that it was worth every penny.

Was it all just a sham or was any of it real?

Tracy said it had been two years that James had been seeing that woman, but Jasmine had seen him with her just before we were married. What was it about her that he couldn't let go of?

It's hard to face the truth to that question, and as I stare at the rug again, I realize that I already know the answer—you can't let go of something you never stopped loving.

Chapter Eighteen

THE WIND IS HOWLING as the rain splashes against the windows of what was once our bedroom. It's funny how in a matter of hours, the weather had turned from sunny and hot to stormy, with lightning so fierce it causes the house to shake.

Is the weather mimicking my life?

Perhaps.

I inhale deeply as I glance at everything in our bedroom except the bed.

A picture of James and me sits on the dresser and as I pick it up and hold it, I can almost feel her hands, and I can see her standing in the same spot I'm in now, staring at this photo encased in a silver frame, imagining herself in it.

I close my eyes as anger seeps into my veins.

When I open them up again, I know that the anger inside of me, has found a home.

The sky is as dark as my heart as I open our closet door, then walk inside, my eyes resting heavily upon his neatly hung suits, and for a split second, it makes me feel like carrying out a scene I once saw in a movie. It's a good thing Jasmine isn't here with me. She would not only encourage me to do something crazy, but she'd also help me.

On the table in the back of the closet sits a hand-carved wooden case holding the many watches I purchased for him over the years. *Ah, he so loved his watches!*

My hand reaches in, pulling out the one with a blue face, the one he was wearing the night I told him I was pregnant. He stopped wearing it, of course, after I had lost the baby.

We went through so much over the years together, but didn't each tribulation only strengthen our love for each other? It seemed so at the time, and it never crossed my mind that I was the only one foolishly feeling that way. Placing the blue watch back inside the case, my fingertips linger upon the red-faced one with a stainless-steel band.

This was the first watch I gave James, purchasing it because it was the same type of watch his father used to have.

One Friday, I had just gotten home from work and found him sitting in the kitchen of our apartment, holding the watch in his open palm, staring at it.

At first, I was going to say something sarcastic, but on seeing the depth of sadness resting on his face, all I could do was move quietly to our bedroom.

He needed to be alone at that moment.

As he climbed into bed, he was wearing the watch. And although the stainless steel was cold against my skin when he wrapped his arms around me, I didn't care.

We did something we hadn't done in a while, talking all night about his parents.

It was then he told me that the watch his father had worn was one his mom bought, and she'd given it to his father for their first anniversary.

James's parents were married over thirty years, living what many would say was a simple life, but his parents had been rich in every way that mattered to James.

Now, it's hard to let how he used to feel about marriage really sink in, now that I know how he treated ours. If someone were to ask me about our marriage today, I'd probably say that James and I had way more than either of our parents did materially, yet we were undoubtedly the poor ones. And that's why they say that love, trust, and faithfulness are worth more than riches.

My phone rings as I ease down onto the carpet. Detective Thompson's name appears on the screen. *Really, honestly, do I want to answer this?* After a couple more rings, I finally hit the answer button.

"Mrs. Reynolds, it's Tracy."

"Hi," I say almost in a whisper, but inside, what I want to say is 'I know it's you, Detective Thompson—or Tracy as you prefer to be called—and I dread every time you call.'"

"Sounds like I caught you at a bad time."

I clear my throat. "Right now, every day is a bad time. What can I do for you, Tracy?"

I know I'm being short with her, and as much as I want to be my old self again, I'm not sure if that woman exists anymore.

My abruptness doesn't seem to faze her.

"I was calling to let you know that your husband's personal items have been released. You can pick them up if you'd like," she says. "Again, it's part of the procedure."

Why don't you just throw them in the trash?

No, I'd probably regret that decision later.

"You still there, Mrs. Reynolds?"

"Yeah, I'm still here. Not that you asked, but I'm here *and* sitting in our closet, trying to convince myself not to burn the house down or just his things."

I sigh as I switch the phone to my other ear.

"I probably shouldn't say such things to you, but since you know how I take my coffee, you'll understand."

The sound of her chuckle, even faintly, manages to pull me out of the dark place into which my thoughts are digging.

"I'm wrapping up for the day, so why don't I bring the things to you?"

"Isn't it still pouring outside?"

"It is, but it's okay. It doesn't make much difference."

"It's funny, but not," I say.

"What is?"

"I was about to give you my address."

"Habit, I'm sure."

"I guess."

"I'll be there in about twenty minutes."

Ending the call, I glance around the closet again and try to push down the anger I feel building up inside of me. My hands dig into the carpet as I think about the moments James and I shared in here. Fighting sometimes, laughing most of the time, and sharing husband and wife moments that I thought would last a lifetime.

Didn't I deserve that?

Jasmine's voice sounds inside my head, telling me to stop asking myself that question because asking it a million times, even aloud, isn't going to give me any answer that I need, and she'd be right. Deep down, it's apparent, but that question seems to follow me.

It's there when I open my eyes, there with each breath. There each time his face appears.

It's impossible to get through a day without it popping into my thoughts.

Walking out of our bedroom, I stop for a second, doing what I told myself I wouldn't do.

I glance over at our bed.

Maybe I'll just burn the sheets.

Chapter Nineteen

JASMINE HAD THE CLEANERS throw everything away from inside the refrigerator; that vacuous shell seems like my life now, empty and worthless.

Leaning up against the counter, the tears well, beginning to fall. Predictable and tedious.

If I were a character in one of my books, the reader would wonder when I was going to get it together, and when I'd dig myself out of this dark hole to see the bright light of life again.

But I'm real. And the hurt I feel is real.

And the light, well the light has faded, barely detectable.

Jasmine said to me just the other day that everyone grieves in different ways. But I doubt that I'm even in the grieving stage. My heart is still filled with too much hatred.

I still have all the grief to come.

I keep hoping that one day I'll wake up and realize this is just a bad dream I'm having. Even now, as I stare at our kitchen table and think about how James and I used to sit at it and have our morning cup of coffee, I want to scream, *Wake up, Raine!*

The reality, however, is that my eyes are wide open, and I'm being forced to live in this nightmare every day. Wherever I look and whatever I do, I'm constantly reminded of the good times. Times I'll never get back.

All I want to do right now is lie down on this kitchen floor and cry until not a tear is left in me. Get every droplet out until the next time.

But I can't because my doorbell is ringing.

"That was a fast twenty minutes," I say. Tracy is standing there, holding a brown paper bag in one hand and two cups of coffee in one of those Styrofoam cup holders in the other.

I know she sees how red and swollen my eyes are, but she doesn't say anything.

"I thought maybe we'd have the coffee first," she says as I reach out and take the cup holder from her, trying to force a smile as I move aside to allow her to step in.

She doesn't look around like most people do when they enter a home. She doesn't need to, I suppose. She knows my home better than I do.

We head to the kitchen, but my eyes still can't move from that bag.

"I can't believe how hard it's raining out there," I say, pulling out a chair and taking a seat. "Such a change from earlier."

She grabs a coffee cup and takes a sip from it.

"Looks like you've been crying harder than it's raining out there," she says, looking over at me, "and I haven't brought my notepad."

"I have plenty of Kleenex, thanks," I say as I give my face a quick wiping, and then grab the other cup of coffee. "How long is this going to last? I mean, you've seen situations like this before. How long does the pain stay in your gut?"

She places her cup of coffee on the table and leans slightly back into her chair. "I don't know if the pain ever really goes away. I think it just becomes so numb, you can't feel it anymore."

"That long, huh?"

She grins and then reaches into her shirt pocket, pulls a business card out, and places it on the table. "I thought you might need this again."

I pick the card up and stare down at it. "How did you know?"

"Because it took me getting that card three times from someone before I actually called it," she says while she straightens up in her chair and then picks her coffee cup back up to take another sip. "This stuff is pretty good. Much better than the stuff we have at the station that I drown myself in daily."

I take a sip of my own coffee, then nod in agreement.

Silence enters the kitchen, and for a couple of minutes, we both enjoy our drinks.

"Tracy, I know it's none of my business… but why did you need to make that call?"

I see her hands wrap themselves around her cup as my question lingers in her mind.

"I guess I needed the same thing you need right now," she finally says.

"A hole to crawl into."

"The card's for when you're ready to crawl out of that hole."

Our eyes shift to the brown paper bag, but when hers meet mine across the table, I see something familiar in them.

Sadness.

Her eyes drop, and she stares down. I sense she's about to say something very painful.

"But to answer your question, about seven years ago, my husband shot and killed our daughter, and then the coward pulled the gun on himself," she says with traces of anger mixed in her tone. "So that's why I acquired the third card."

I almost gag. "Sorry, I wasn't expecting that," I say as I fight to get my composure back. "I'm so sorry for your loss."

"Me, too. It happened on a Friday. A code 55-A had come in—that means that it's a homicide. But I had no idea that it was a homicide that would affect me. Affect my life or my sanity, if I'm being completely candid. There I was, sitting at my desk, trying to get some paperwork done that I was behind on. I wasn't a detective back then. But I was gunning for it as they say, so it was normal for me to still be at the station even when my shift had ended.

"When the Chief called me into his office at 6:30 to tell me, at first, I thought it was some kind of joke, but the look on his face told me it was real.

"I could barely breathe. In all honesty, I think my heart must have stopped beating," she says, looking over at me. "You know what I mean?"

I nod, knowing exactly what she means.

"After I left the Chief's office, I went back to my desk and just sat there, trying to process everything. I must have sat there for at least an hour before my body could move.

"When I finally arrived at the scene, my husband and daughter's bodies had already been taken from the house itself but were still outside, waiting to be loaded up. Uniforms were everywhere.

Many of them I knew from the station. No one could look me in the eye as I walked over to my daughter's body."

She pauses, swallowing the building lump in her throat.

"I could tell you exactly what my girl had on that day. Her hair was still in the ponytail I had put it in before leaving for work. All I can say to you, Mrs. Reynolds, is to be thankful that you were out of town. Seeing the body of your loved one like that, your own child, is something that lives with you forever. It alters everything, for the rest of your life."

I don't know what to say to her, but I agree that going through what I'm going through now would have been harder had I actually seen James's body.

"I know I said this already, Tracy, but again, I'm so sorry." It doesn't come out the way it should, almost in a whisper, because I'm sitting here, barely able to keep it together.

Her pain taps into my pain.

"We'd been married ten years and had just purchased our first home, not too far from here," she says after letting out a deep sigh. "My husband's name was Matthew. He was a stockbroker, and our little girl's name was Matty. We met at a grocery store, Matthew and I. He was smart and handsome and could make me laugh. I mean, like really laugh, and you need that in your life when you're a police officer."

I nod, giving the simplest encouragement but not interrupting.

"I asked myself 'why' a million times, as I'm sure you've done, if not still doing it."

My head slowly nods again.

"You feel like knowing the 'why' will somehow help you process it better. Deal with it better. It's been seven years, and not a day goes by when I don't want the answer to that question.

But here's what I've learned, Mrs. Reynolds, here's what calling the person on that card taught me… That life can go on *without ever knowing the answer.*

"Sounds impossible, I know. I'm not saying it's easy, but I learned to breathe, learned to do more than just move and exist. It was hard, every day a struggle. But in time, I could smell the roses and appreciate them when I passed by some, if that makes any sense."

"It does," I say softly.

"When I tell you that making that call saved me, I mean it with every fiber of my being. In the beginning, I didn't just crawl into a hole. No, I dug myself into one so deep that I couldn't see the light anymore. And I kept digging. And to be honest, before I made that call, I didn't want to see the light. My daughter had been my illumination. She was only two years old. And when that light was stolen away, I questioned what was left to live for."

I place the card on the table and reach over, settling my hand on top of hers. "Did you hate him for it? I think that's where I'm at now. The hatred bit."

"When all the light is taken away from you, all you have is hate. But here's the other thing I learned. Hatred can eat at you. It can live and breathe in your gut. It can become your heartbeat if you let it. Or if it doesn't become it, then it devours it. Either way, it takes you over."

Her words find a space in my thoughts. I remove my hand and pick the card back up again.

"Don't worry, Mrs. Reynolds, if you tear that one up or throw it in the trash, I have a couple more ready."

A chuckle slips out just as a few more tears fall.

Moving her chair back, she picks up her coffee cup and then stands.

Both of our eyes move in the direction of that paper bag.

"I'll get going," she says, looking down at me. "And again, consider making that call."

I push my chair back and stand up as well. "Thank you for coming and bringing me James's things, Tracy. I know you didn't have to make the trip, especially on such a wretched day."

"What will you do with the house?" she asks as we make our way toward the front door.

"I'm going to sell it," I say, opening the door and seeing the rain coming down even harder. "Do you want me to get you an umbrella?"

She looks up and smiles. "The rain and I became best friends a long time ago."

I smile, though unsure what she means by that. "Tracy, I hope you don't mind me asking this, but what did you do with your home?"

"I burned it down," she says, stepping outside. And she says it as though it's absolutely the truth, yet there's a slight pull at her lips as though she might grin. "But if you ever tell anyone I admitted that to you, I'll deny it."

Chapter Twenty

I KNOW I'VE BEEN standing in the kitchen, staring at it, long enough. Staring at the brown paper bag holding the last things James had on him that fatal night that took him away from me.

I say that, but if I'm honest with myself, it seems I lost him way before that night. Only I didn't know it. Or why.

My feet move toward the table, my heart beating so fast it makes me nervous, but I don't stop moving until I have the brown paper bag in my hand.

Holding the bag in my hand feels weird.

It feels like loneliness.

How can a brown paper bag feel like loneliness? I guess in the sense that the owner of the contents within it is gone. Placing the bag on the counter, I take a deep breath and then open it.

I pull out his watch, the brown one with a gold band, the one he bought a couple of months ago. Placing the watch on the counter, I reach back inside.

My fingers feel his leather wallet, so I pull it out, wanting to open it, but finding I can't.

What if there's a picture of him and her inside?

I place the wallet down on the counter, unopened, and step back. "Just get it over with," I say aloud, moving back to the counter and picking up the wallet. A letter falls out of it.

It's from her. Has to be.

> *James,*
>
> *I'm sending you this letter because you won't talk to me. It's a shame that I had to make this letter look like a legal document to ensure you'd open it. I've called your office several times, but your gatekeeper gives me the usual pitch of "he's out of the office with a client."*
>
> *You and I both know that not talking to each other isn't going to make the situation go away.*
>
> *I'm not going to lie, I almost texted you, but didn't as you know.*
>
> *We agreed not to ever text each other, but if you don't take my calls at your office, you're going to force me to take that route. Please don't make me do that. We're both grown here.*
>
> *We both knew the risks.*
>
> *You're acting like this is all my fault, but I promise you, I'm not going to let you blow me off.*

Because, most of all, I love you.

I've loved you since the first day we met in college. My love for you never wavered even when you left me for her. Even when you married her. Even when you bought her that huge house.

You gave her the life I should have been living. That we, together, should have been living. You know how my heart beats for you, so I can't understand how you can treat me this way. And I don't understand how you can claim not to love me.

So, tell me, James, what did the last two years mean?

If you really loved that woman you call your wife, then why were you with me every time she was away? You didn't seem to be so in love with her when we were together.

I don't deserve this and I'm definitely not raising this child without you, so it's time to man up and tell wifey that you're leaving her for me. I mean it, James!

It's not me or her this time. It can only be me. It can only be us and our child.

Don't you get that?

Can't you see that?

I need you to see that.

I know she's out of town this weekend, so I'll come by your house, and we can sit down and discuss how you're going to tell her that you want a divorce.

Please believe that if you don't, I will.

This child, your child, deserves to have you in its life, not just child support or weekend visits.

I've waited long enough. It's time for you and me to finally be together.

Don't make me mad.

Don't tell me again that you're not leaving her.

I'm not listening to that foolishness anymore.

I'll see you tonight.

Love always and forever,
Monica.

Chapter Twenty-One

"WELL, SHE WAS A piece of work," Jasmine says as she leans back into her blue velvet sofa. The letter dangles in her hand as I sit across from her. "Do you want to go into my kitchen and burn this?" she asks, handing the letter back to me as though it's laced with poison.

I guess, in a way, it is.

I take a sip of my wine before grabbing hold of it with the tips of my fingers. "Burning this garbage isn't going to make me feel better."

"True, but it would make me feel better," she says as the tears begin to make their way down the sides of my face.

She reaches behind her, grabbing a box of Kleenex from her side table, handing it to me.

"Thanks," I say, putting my wine on the coffee table, then grabbing a handful of tissues out of the box. "I feel like you have a box of these in every room of your house just for me."

"I picked up a case this morning," she says with a slight smirk.

"Thank you."

"So, did you finally decide what to do with the house? You already know what I propose."

I lean back into the sofa and let out a soft sigh. "I'm going to sell it, not burn it down. What's up with you wanting to burn everything?"

"I don't know. Fire just ensures it doesn't come back. Who wants the bad stuff back in their life? I sure don't. Once it's gone, it's gone. That's my motto."

It seems as if something is hidden in her words, but I can't put my finger on it.

"Let's put it on the market. There's no way I could ever live in it again. Do you have an agent in mind?"

"I do. I met a real estate agent in New York, but he moved here about six months ago. I reached out to him and told him to be on standby. He's already pulled the comps, so he's ready to get things started as soon as possible."

"What would I do without you?"

"I'm glad neither of us has to find out. Now, what are you going to do about yourself?"

My eyebrows rise. "What do you mean?"

"Are you going to try and start writing again?"

I grab my wine glass and take a sip. "I don't know. Honestly, I'm not sure about anything right now. The only decision I've made besides selling the house is to go and see this shrink that the detective referred me to."

"They do help. If you get the right one, put it that way. Bad ones can screw you up."

"A bit like men then. Husbands," I say, attempting a badly timed quip.

I look at her and see something around the corner of her eyes, a pain I've never seen before; is it something new or something that I just never noticed before?

"What's going on with you?"

She stares across the room as if looking into a window of the past.

My hand reaches over, then lies atop her shoulder. "What is it, Jasmine?"

"What do you mean?" She tries to hide it with a smile, but it doesn't reach her eyes. And I know Jasmine better than anyone. I know when she is someplace else.

"There's something you're not telling me."

"It's nothing... I'm fine. Really. I just think it's a positive step."

"Come on. No more secrets between us, please."

Her bottom lip quivers at the words, and for a moment, she just breathes before pulling the revelation from her throat. "I didn't leave New York just because I wanted to start my own business here, and it was cheaper. I left because I'd been attacked."

I place my hand over my mouth.

"Raped, actually. I never told anyone, not even my parents or you," she says, looking over at me. "At first, I don't know whether it was because I was embarrassed that it happened or because I blamed myself for it happening. I mean, it was my fault somehow. I'm sure of it."

"I don't know the details, but there's no way you should take the blame for something as horrific as that. None of us walk around wearing signs saying, 'hurt me!'"

She fringes a smile, but the tears that fall tell me she's still struggling with it.

"It was a co-worker," she says, taking another sip of her wine. "No," she says, after pausing for a second. "Look, Raine; I'm not going to hide a single thing from you. Because we are friends, right? And you don't hide things from me but just bear in mind how embarrassed and uncomfortable I am."

She almost weeps. Almost. "Hey," I say. "Be strong. Because you *can* be strong. You've been my rock for so long, so I know your strength better than anyone else in the world. But when you need to lean on me, I'm going to be *your* rock, all right?"

She smiles. A little. Her eyes are watery, filling up.

"The monster who did that to me was more than just a co-worker. It was my boss."

"Oh, no."

"And I'm so ashamed…" she says.

"There's no need. He abused you. Abused his position, everything!" I reassure her.

"Exactly." She picks up her wine glass and twirls it nervously in her hand. "He had a thing for me and that much was obvious, but I never thought it would come to that. Never thought—"

I reach over again and place my hand on her shoulder. "You don't have to tell me the details."

She places her glass of wine down and then reaches behind her to grab a few tissues out of the Kleenex box. "I guess you're not the only one that needs these."

"You know what they say, misery loves company."

She nods as she dabs the corners of her eyes.

"It happened so fast."

"You really don't have to talk about it, Jasmine."

"No, I should have told you about it a long time ago. It'd be better to share it."

I pick up the wine bottle and pour some into our glasses.

"You can fill mine to the top, please."

"In that case, I'll fill both of ours up."

I smile, but as she lifts her glass to the brim of her lips, her hands are trembling.

"Where was I?"

"You were saying that it happened quickly," I say, picking up my wine glass, and then taking a quick sip.

"Yeah, that's right." Her eyes shift downward, and she stares into the wine for a minute or two.

"We were both working late one night. Trying to put together a last-minute marketing strategy for a book that wasn't doing well. One minute, I was talking about how I thought the book just needed a little more time in the market, and the next minute, he was—"

Her glass begins to shake.

"That night is forever etched into my memory. Even today, at this very second, I can tell you what kind of stinking cologne he had on that day, and while the darkness doesn't visit me as much as it used to after it first happened, I can still feel it in the corners of my mind."

We both take a couple more sips of wine.

"Jasmine?"

"Yeah."

"Did you ever report it?"

She doesn't say anything. Her eyes have this haze over them.

"Jasmine?"

She shakes her head slowly as I stare at her in disbelief.

"Don't look at me like that. Don't judge me."

"I'm not judging you. I'm just surprised. He could do it to someone else. Every attack needs to be reported."

She raises her glass, but then stops. "He did do it to someone else. It happened about six years later. Maybe a touch longer."

"How do you know? That he attacked someone else, I mean?"

"By then, I was working for another PR agency, but the case had made it into the paper. The lady he attacked not only brought charges against him, but she also sued the publishing company. Apparently, there'd been other complaints against him, but the company failed to investigate."

"I remember that. I remember she won that case and a boatload of money because an ex-employee had stepped forward as well. Was that you?"

Jasmine nods.

"It wasn't easy. Seeing him in court every day was like reliving that day over and over again. When the trial ended, I moved here and opened up my PR agency. But the hardest part of all wasn't being in that courtroom with him. No, the hardest part had come way before the trial or the case against him, for that matter."

I sit up. "How so?"

"I'd gotten pregnant."

I try not to gasp as she takes a big sip of her wine.

"Before you ask, I put the baby up for adoption. It was a boy."

"After I gave birth to him, they tried to bring him to me, but I wouldn't let them. I wasn't trying to be cruel; it wasn't his fault, but I just couldn't go there. At that time, the pain was still too fresh. I'd lived with it for nine months, and to be honest, I thought that after I had the baby, after he was no longer in my life, the pain would go away but it didn't. That's when I went to see a therapist." She releases a deep, shaky breath. "My company paid for it, and I went for about three years."

"I'm so sorry, Jasmine. I hate that I wasn't there for you when you needed me most."

"You didn't know."

"I really wish I *had* known. I can't imagine anyone going through all of that by themselves. I mean, look at me. I wouldn't have been able to deal with everything that's happening to me right now if I didn't have my best friend by my side."

"We've both been through so much, haven't we?"

I nod my head. "Yeah, we have."

"Good thing I have more wine. And tissues. Let's not forget those."

We both laugh, but the tears haven't cleared completely for either of us.

"What was it like seeing the shrink?" I ask after a few minutes pass.

She sits up. "It was scary at first. It's hard to tell someone, especially a stranger, the things that you can't tell anyone else. Things that you can't even discuss with your best friend. The things you don't want to admit to yourself even. But after time, it gets easier to open up. They have a way of easing you into trusting them."

"What didn't you want to admit to yourself?"

She lets out a long sigh. "That I hated him."

"Your boss? That's understandable surely."

"The baby."

She looks over at me to see if I have a reaction to her revelation, but I don't. How could I? While my situation is tragic, her story is a different kind of tragedy altogether and one she's hidden so well. Hers is the kind of tragedy who'll grow up one day and wonder who his real parents are. Not that I'm calling her son a tragedy—no child is that—but he was born as a result of one, and he'll have to carry this all the days of his life.

"Do you still hate him?"

She looks pensive, perhaps a little distant.

"It took a long time for me to direct my hatred toward the person who really deserved it. When I was pregnant, I did everything the doctor told me to do, and I prayed the baby didn't feel my hatred, and if he did, I hoped that he'd forgive me. I know that sounds weird."

I shake my head no. "Not at all."

"In my mind, he didn't deserve it. He deserved a beautiful life, but I couldn't give that to him. Even if I wanted to do so, it just wasn't in me to give because of the association and damage that man caused to me. It was going to take me years to work through it."

"Do you ever think about looking for him?"

"I've had my moments over the years. I would see a little boy while walking and think to myself, he should be about that age. Or there'd be a father playing with his son, and I would hope that my son had plenty of moments like that. And just when you feel something like regret, you remember. And just like that, the moment is gone. Sounds harsh, doesn't it?"

"No. It sounds truthful to me."

"There's always that chance the child I gave birth to will come looking for me, and if that happens, I can only hope that I'd have the courage to face him."

"Will you tell him, do you think? I know that's hard to answer because—"

She cuts me off mid-flow. "I won't tell him, no! I know how hard it is to deal with a situation like that. I wouldn't put him through it."

"What if he insists?"

"Then I'll lie."

Chapter Twenty-Two

I'VE BEEN EXPECTING TO pull up to an office building, but instead, my GPS directs me to a quiet, but older residential neighborhood in Alpharetta.

After rechecking the address, I turn the car off and lean back into my seat, my eyes resting on the pale blue Victorian-style home in front of me with a wraparound porch that spans from the front of the home to a corner on the right, where there's a nice red door and two rocking chairs.

I'm assuming the red door leads to his office.

Two more rocking chairs sit to the left of the screened front door. I admire how they're ready to provide anyone sitting in them with a measure of comfort and a chance to rock away any worries. Not too many things today can accomplish that.

The front yard is filled with plants and flowers, so I assume he likes to garden. Or maybe his wife does. Either way, it's impressive.

A bird flies by my window and finds a resting place on the edge of the birdhouse hanging from the white gingerbread trim.

It's a cardinal. And quite beautiful.

It pays me no mind as it pulls bird seed into its beak. A few seconds later, it looks my way, and I get the sense that it's telling me it's okay to finally get out of my car.

I glance at the mailbox. D. Carter is inscribed on the side of it.

You don't see mailboxes like that anymore.

I'm not sure what that tells me about the person who lives in the house or bears that name. And I wonder what the D stands for.

Taking a deep breath, I open my car door and step out, gripping my car keys like a security blanket. My heels dig into the dirt, the wet grass touching my toes as I make my way to the sidewalk, and then up the walkway to the front steps.

A sign tells me to come in through the red door, so I move in that direction.

As I open the door, an older woman with hair as smooth as silk says hello.

Her voice alone reminds me of my mother, and I can't help but think that if my mother were still living, the two of them could have been twins in kindness.

"You must be Raine Reynolds," she says as she walks around the intricately carved desk behind which she was sitting.

"I am," I say shyly, but not sure why. "I'm so sorry I'm late."

The width of her smile causes my shoulders to relax.

"You're not late, dear. Your appointment isn't for another five minutes. I always give someone new a twenty-minute head start. You're not the first person to sit outside and contemplate whether they want to come in or not," she says with a wink.

"Smart," I say, putting my keys into my purse.

She points to a gray sofa with big yellow pillows on it, so I walk over and take a seat. "This is a beautiful home."

"It is," she says, sitting beside me and crossing her legs. "This house has been in this neighborhood for over a century. Everyone was so happy when Dr. Carter purchased it. It was a real dump before then as they say."

"It looks like it's being well taken care of now."

"Trust me, it is. Dr. Carter restored the outside over the years to match the original design but went with a more modern feel for the inside. It was in one of those home décor magazines, about three years ago. They did a great story on it. Showed it in its true glory. Maybe after your next session's over, I'll give you a tour."

"You don't have to do that, but I'd love to see the rest of the house."

"I don't mind; I love showing off this house. One would think it were my own."

"Well, you certainly add to its warmth. I am curious about something. Why did you say that you'll show me around after my next session?"

She glances down at her watch, then back up at me with a smile. "Dr. Carter will be finished in another minute or two. By the way, I'm Ruth McGuire, but Dr. Carter calls me Ruthie."

"That's a nice name," I say, sensing that she isn't going to answer my question.

"It is and it isn't. I wasn't crazy about it, but over the years, I've learned to accept the *old woman* name my mother gave me. Especially now that I *am* an old woman."

"You remind me of my mother," I say, glancing around, admiring the intricate trim work.

Ruthie's eyes follow mine. "Dr. Carter installed that trim himself. He's quite handy. I often tell him that if he decides to leave this profession, Home Depot would hire him in a second."

I can't help but laugh.

"He opened this office right after completing his fellowship. Why anyone in their right mind would want to go to school for twelve long years and then do a fellowship after that is beyond me." She glances down at her watch again. "I was one of his first patients. I came here for two solid years after the loss of my daughter, and then I started working for him. I say all that so that you know how good he is. You don't come work for someone who isn't."

"I can agree with that," I say, just as a door opens and a woman walks out.

Ruthie stands up and walks over to her. I watch as they chat for a second before Ruthie walks her to the red door.

I feel a slight tremble in my knees.

Ruthie walks over and sits next to me again, reaching out, placing her hand on my knee. "I could tell you not to be nervous, but that's always the easiest thing to say in a situation like this. Just remember, he won't bite and certainly won't kill you."

She gives me another wink and then stands back up.

"Come on, I'll take you in. Dr. Carter may have stepped into the main house for a few minutes, but he'll be right back. He likes to refresh his cup of tea in between patients. I've offered to do it for him a million times, but he insists on doing himself."

I stand up, straighten out the black skirt I'm wearing, and then follow her into a room filled with beautifully placed antiques and books with ragged edges, gracing shelves made from solid oak. "This doesn't look the way I imagined it would," I say after taking a minute to tour the room with my eyes.

"There's no couch," a male voice says.

I turn around and stare into the eyes of a man I met over fifteen years ago.

Donovan.

Chapter Twenty-Three

"I REMEMBER YOU," I say as he walks over to me. "A bit taller than I remember." His eyebrows rise. "My friend Jasmine and I were just graduating from college, and you were with a young guy at the time—James Reynolds? Do you remember it? Time flies…! We were all at a Waffle House, and the two of you had just graduated from law school!"

His deep hazel brown eyes light up as that day at the Waffle House returns to him.

"James Reynolds! Now, that's a name I haven't heard in years," he says as I follow him over to a pair of chairs sitting by the window. "But I wasn't graduating from law school."

He offers me a chair, and I catch a slight whiff of his cologne, the woodsy aroma reminding me of a carefree walk in the forest.

Ruthie walks out of the room and gently closes the door behind her.

After we both take a seat, I ask, "So, how do you know James, then?" He places his cup of tea on a small table next to his chair.

"I didn't really. I'd gone to the school to pick someone up, but they'd already left. James and I met by accident. Literally. Like—*crash!* And our cars got to know each other!"

"Wow."

"I was pulling out of a parking space when the front of his bumper hit the side of mine. It wasn't serious, but he insisted on taking me to grab something to eat by way of making it up to me. To be honest, I had no idea we were going to a Waffle House!" he says.

"Not really your type of restaurant, I take it."

"Not really," he says with a grin that allows a dimple in his right cheek to reveal itself.

He leans back and I can see how broad his shoulders are as he places his cup down on the table again. "Come to think of it, I do remember you and him arguing over French fries. You two seemed to hit it off pretty good."

"We did," I say, trying to hide the bitterness in my voice. "Well, I believed we did. No, we really did," I voice, confusing even myself. "I never knew about the accident. James never mentioned it." I pause for a second, placing my hands on my lap. "We were married."

"That's amazing! You only read about stuff like that—an instant attraction that leads to something. But is that why you came to see me? Are you finding the divorce difficult?"

"How do you know we aren't still married?"

"You stated that you *were* married."

He's better than a detective at this… "Well spotted," I say quietly. My enthusiasm has left.

I glance out the window as the trembling in my knees returns. Donovan's gaze is watching me, but he says nothing until, "I'm sorry. Did my comment unsettle you? It's a habit of psychotherapists. Sometimes, we speak our minds, but I'd really like you to do it too."

"Your yard is beautiful," I say, giving myself a moment to breathe. "Your wife must love to garden. It must take up so much time to keep it in such good shape."

"You'll have to thank Ruthie for that. She spends an hour or two out there after we finish the day. It's something she enjoys, and as you've just proven, it gives a more homey feel."

"Free therapy," I say with a smile simpler than I would have liked.

"Something like that, I suppose."

His eyes are kind, and it's strange because I feel as though another man's eyes haven't made any impression on me in over fifteen years, and I'm not sure why now I decide to linger.

"How long did the marriage last?"

"Well, I might have said that it lasted right up to the point that his mistress killed him earlier this summer, but now I'd say that it lasted right up to the point that he decided to sleep with her. So, before you ask, yes, that's why I'm here. Because I need help."

"Help with what?"

"Dealing with his death or help with dealing with the affair. Maybe, a bit of both, I suppose."

He leans forward and stares into my eyes. "I see."

"What is it that you *see*, Dr. Carter?" I ask, a little annoyed.

"Only Ruthie calls me Dr. Carter."

"Okay," I say, straightening my skirt even though it doesn't need it. "What is it that you see me suffering from, Donovan?"

He again looks me in the eyes with an intensity that makes me sit up straighter in my chair. "I cannot tell you what you are 'suffering from'. That's more of a medical term, as in disease, viruses and so on. But I sense you've come because you want to get rid of the hatred that's here." My knees go from trembling to shaking out of control as he places his hand on his heart.

"How do you know that?" I ask.

"I can hear it."

"You can't hear what's in my heart. You might be a good shrink, I mean, psychotherapist, psychiatrist, or whatever it is, but I'm sure you're not that good."

"I heard it when you said, *we were married*."

I stand up, walk over to the window, and place my hand on the pane as I look out. "You know what I see out of here?"

"Something that you want, perhaps?"

"How did you know that?" I ask, as my hand drops to my side.

"The way you placed your hand on the window. For just a moment, your body relaxed."

"That's what I see out there."

"Relaxation?"

"No. Peacefulness. I want that so badly, but I know the only way I'm going to get it is by being completely honest."

"With yourself, or me?"

"Both, maybe."

I want some sort of response, but he says nothing.

A soft September breeze bounces off the glazing. "I do hate him. But I don't just hate *him*—I hate her, not just because she took his life, but because she wanted mine as well."

"You mean she wanted the life you had with James?"

I turn around and face him. "Yes, but it was more than that."

"How so?"

"She felt that the life James and I had never should have come to fruition. She resented me because he married me."

"How do you know that?"

"I read it in a letter that she wrote to him that was in his wallet. I noticed it when the police released his belongings a few days after."

He motions for me to sit back down, and I do.

"You asked how long our marriage lasted and I gave you one side of the truth. The other side is that we were married for what I thought were fifteen years of honesty, love, and trust."

"And now you feel that honesty and trust didn't exist for those fifteen years?"

"Yes. But neither did love."

"I can't say I agree with that."

"How could you not agree with that? He had a mistress!"

"True, but you just told me the mistress resented that he married you instead of her."

"I don't understand your point."

"Were you rich, or were your parents rich?"

"No, not even a little, and neither was my father. Why?"

"Then you know that he didn't marry you for money, so it must have been for something else, right?"

I lean back in my chair. "Right."

Walking to my car, I stop to look back at the red door that I had been afraid to walk through an hour and a half ago. As I pull my keys out of my purse, I feel something.

Hope. It's faint, but I know that it's there.

The mailbox catches my attention again as I slip the key in the ignition and begin to maneuver out. Who knew that D. Carter would stand for Dr. Donovan Carter?

Glancing in the rearview mirror, the mailbox begins to fade out of view, but there's a smile on my face that doesn't seem to want to go away. I must admit that it feels good to use those cheek muscles again.

Chapter Twenty-Four

IT'S AMAZING HOW QUICKLY the weather shifts in September. The mornings, of course, bring in cooler temperatures, but on nights like tonight, with the windows of my car down and the radio playing a good mix of Jazz and R&B, I welcome the warmth as hints of a gentle breeze tickle my skin. I even feel like sticking my hand out the window and allowing the breeze to sink deep into my bones as I move it to the beat of the music. What's ironic, is that this morning, over coffee, Jasmine commented that I look as though I'm finally coming out of my *fog* of despair.

Perhaps she's right. Something's different. That feeling of hope that I felt after my first session with Donovan is still lingering inside me.

I can't believe I'm looking forward to my next session tomorrow.

Maybe I need to do my sessions twice a week, instead of weekly.

I continue to ponder over that possibility as I hit the expressway, eager to make it downtown in thirty minutes, if possible, to meet Jasmine and her parents, Vicky and Jack, for dinner.

Of course, Jasmine thinks I'm only looking forward to my next session because, as she put it, "Donovan is extremely handsome." My words, not hers.

That girl is a mess, but I'm so thankful for her.

Just as I finally make it off the expressway, my phone rings. "I knew you'd be calling me," I say as I make my way over to the left lane. "Before you get on me for being late, I'm less than ten minutes out." A car darts in front of me, and I hit the brakes. "Hey, are you there?" I hear a voice, but it's so low. "Jasmine, are you there?"

"Raine, it's Vicky, Jasmine's mother."

"Vicky. Sorry, I thought you were Jasmine."

"I'm calling you from her phone."

"Why? Is everything all right?"

"Can you pull over?"

"I'm about to make a turn. What's wrong?"

"I need you to pull over first." I can hear the trembling in her voice.

"Tell me what's going on."

"Please, Raine. Just pull over."

"Give me a minute. I'll call you right back."

"Okay."

Panic is setting in as I pull into the lot of a closed gas station. The smell of gasoline fills my nostrils, and I take a few deep breaths before dialing Vicky back.

"Raine?"

"Yeah, it's me. What in the world is going on?"

"I-I don't know how to tell you this, I can't believe it myself, b-but Jasmine is gone."

"Gone? What do you mean, gone? Gone where?"

"She was getting inside her car when she was hit by a car. She was… our girl is gone, Raine. She was killed instantly."

I can't stop my hands from shaking as I hold the phone to my ear.

"Raine, are you there, honey?"

"Yes," is all I manage to whisper as tears flood my cheeks.

Chapter Twenty-Five

FIVE YEARS LATER

I can't believe how hard the rain is coming down as my cab pulls up to a sixteen-story building.

No one should be intimated by mere bricks and mortar, but it's not the building itself causing a slight tremor to ride up my spine. It's more about what it represents.

And that's coming back to a place I doubt will ever feel like home again.

The rain beats heartily on the cab's roof, and I know the cab driver wishes I would get over whatever has me still sitting in his cab more than two minutes after pulling up.

This fact is confirmed when he glances in his rear-view mirror at my fear-stricken face and asks if I need help getting my luggage out.

"No," I say, as I finally open the door, open my umbrella too, and drag my luggage and fear with me to the revolving doors.

The cab driver pulls off quickly without a second glance back in my direction.

The moment the doors start to move, I feel as though I'm stepping back into the past.

"You must be Raine?"

I nod apprehensively at a tall woman with red hair styled in a shoulder-length bob. Her navy skirt barely covers everything important, and her V-neck blouse exposes everything that's most important. But her confident smile could fill the foyer of the building. "It's so good to finally meet you face to face. How was your flight from Paris?" Briana, my real estate agent, asks.

"Over nine hours, but I'm glad to make it safely," I say just as we head toward the elevators.

"I've never been to Paris, but I hear it's breathtaking. Lots of beautiful and romantic places to explore," she says as the elevator doors slide open.

"Yes, Paris has plenty of those," I say, pulling my luggage into the elevator.

"I'm sure they do. I've watched that movie *Sabrina* a million times. She found herself in Paris, she said in the movie, or something like that."

"What floor are we going to?" I ask, as the elevator doors close swiftly.

"Sorry." She hits the button for the tenth floor. "Will you miss it? Paris, I mean?"

"Sure." I can't help but notice how much younger she looks in person than the photo I saw of her on the real estate website. I peg her around twenty-three, which means I was in my second year of college when she was born. I'm not sure why that bothers me, but it does.

"I hear Paris is filled with beautiful gardens, which reminds me, the unit we're about to see provides access to the roof, where you'll find an amazing garden. Do you garden?"

"I don't, unfortunately."

"My mother loves to garden. She says that it brings her a sense of peace and quietness in her life."

I glance over the elevator door display to see which floor we're on, praying that the elevator moves as swiftly as the doors closed.

"I can't wait to show you this unit. If I could afford it, I'd live in it myself."

I give her a wry smile. "The pictures you emailed were nice."

"Personally, I don't think pictures do this place justice. But you can be the judge of that. Did I mention that the building has a nice gym? Do you enjoy working out?"

"Not really," I say as the elevator doors finally open. I feel a touch sorry for her. She's trying to point out all the added reasons to enthuse about this place, and she's not hooking me. I don't garden. Don't exercise. *What else will she hope I indulge in? Now, if the apartment came with a massive larder stocked with luscious food and wine... then we'd have a lot to talk about.*

"I wouldn't know what to do with myself if I didn't start each day with a three-mile jog on my treadmill. It really helps me focus for the rest of the day. You should try it, but then again, you don't look like you need to exercise. I hope I look like you when I'm your age. Do you need a hand with your luggage?"

My age?

I step out of the elevator with my luggage in tow. "It's just the one. The rest of my things will come later if things go well here."

Her eyebrows rise slightly, but then quickly rest with a smile that forms. "I'm quite sure you're going to love this unit. It's just down the hall."

As I follow her down the hall, every part of me wants to run back to Paris. Did I *find* myself like Sabrina did in the movie? Yes, but I wasn't going to mention that to Briana.

Why did you let yourself get talked into coming back here?

"How long have you been away from Georgia?" she asks as we step into the foyer of a fully furnished two-bedroom condo.

"Five years." I place my luggage in the corner by the door.

"Well, welcome back. You're going to love living in Alpharetta."

You don't say...

"Are you familiar with the area?"

"I've been out here, but it was years ago." A picture of a Victorian-styled home with a red door enters my mind.

"This area's really grown, taken off, you know? Urbanization, becoming one of the best areas to live. There are so many restaurants within a mile or so from here and the mall's just a few miles away as well. Are you a shopper like I am?"

"I'm not." Oh dear. Another miss. If that sounds short, she doesn't seem to notice.

"My mother hates to shop too, so I get it. Before I forget to mention it, there's a great coffee shop just around the corner; it's next to the dog park. You do drink coffee, right?"

"I prefer tea, actually."

"On that note then, let's start in the kitchen. The floors in the kitchen are dark brown, but unlike the top-of-the-line hardwoods of this foyer, the kitchen floors are made from premium waterproof engineered hardwood. I think they did a fabulous job making sure you can't tell the difference. You'll see what I mean."

I glance down at the foyer's floor, but only because it seems obvious that she is expecting me to, and then I follow her into the kitchen.

There was a time when I noticed things like that, but I'm not that person anymore.

"Don't you just love these ceiling-high navy-blue cabinets? I think the brass door handles, marble countertops, and matching brass sink faucet really make things in this kitchen pop."

"It is very nice." I'm struggling to bring myself to her level of excitement over the kitchen. I didn't sleep much last night, and I didn't get to eat anything before jumping on an 8 a.m. flight.

And I almost missed that! But if I'm being honest with myself, the almost missed flight may have been a little intentional.

"If you look to your right, you'll find a coffee machine with a hot water button for your tea. I'm a coffee shop kind of girl myself."

"The appliances look new," I say to move the conversation along and hopefully to the next room to check out.

"The Koch stainless-steel appliances were installed a few months ago, along with the brass hooded vent above the stove. Do you cook?"

Oh goodness. Here we go again. Another no.

I try to vary this one a little.

"It's only me, so I don't cook much. But I don't mind it now and then. The only thing I would probably use in here is that hot water button."

Her eyes quickly blink, and she shifts slightly. "Who knows, maybe this kitchen will help spark the chef in you, but if not, like I stated earlier, there are plenty of restaurants nearby."

"I'm all about takeout," I say with a good smile, my small effort to redeem myself from the sarcastic comment about the hot water button.

A smile cradles her face. "I love to cook. To me, the kitchen is the most important space in a home. And this… well this would be just perfect."

I want to tell her that any room that allows me to kick off the three-inch heels I foolishly have on, pour myself a glass of wine, and soak in a tub, is the most important space in a home to me. But I say nothing as we finally move from the kitchen and into the master bedroom, where she walks me through the huge walk-in closet with custom built-ins and then on to the bathroom that's big enough to hold an arsenal of towels.

"What do you think? Doesn't it look better than the pictures I sent you?"

"It looks very nice," I say, trying not to yawn. "I like all of it."

She claps her hands, and for a moment, I can't tell whether I'm dealing with a real estate agent or a high school cheerleader.

"I knew you would. Let's move down the hallway toward the living room. I can't wait to show you the view of the city skyline from there. It's so inspiring."

The moment we reach the living room, huge bay windows greet me, and I find myself staring out at a sky that's so calm my shoulders relax the longer I stare at it.

James mentioned that a view like this was the one thing he didn't get in the home we shared.

Why are you going there, Raine? I glance back out the bay windows again and try my best not to see his face staring back at me. *Why are you spending time thinking about a man you've given yourself five years to forget?*

"How much did you say the lease is for this property?" I say to force my mind back into the present. I don't really care what it costs; I'm not the one paying for it.

"It's four thousand a month, but the owner is also open to selling it if you're interested."

"I'm not sure if I'm ready to buy anything, but I am interested in leasing it for now."

I see a hint of disappointment, but she reaches inside her purse and pulls out a folder with a rental agreement inside it.

"I can't imagine not wanting to own a place like this. You must travel a lot, do you?"

"I used to travel quite often. The ad agency that I work for now doesn't require it. But since I used to live in Georgia, they sent me here to head up our creative development and design department."

"That sounds exciting, but I'm sure running an entire department is demanding."

"The 'demanding' part of my job keeps me distracted. I mean, busy."

"Have you always been in that line of work?"

I can't put my finger on it to be sure, but the way she asks the question makes me think she already knows the answer.

"I worked for an agency for a few years after college, but then I tried something else for a while. I went back to the ad life about five years ago."

"And you're already a senior VP. That's great."

"That happens when all you have in your life is work."

"Real estate is my life, as well. My mother says that I'm married to it. She's right. I love what I do. But we need to do what we're passionate about? Don't you agree?"

She stares at me, her eyes searching through me as though they're trying to draw something out of me, and I'm not ready to dig down into the well of my darkest secrets and tell them to a real estate agent. A really intrusive one, though she's pleasant enough.

"I don't believe you have to be passionate about work if you like it enough to show up each day and not kill yourself. I learned that in Paris."

She cackles with laughter.

"Do you have a pen?" I ask, eager to get the agreement signed so I can finally relax, and she can leave.

"Of course. Do you want to step into the dining room to sign it? It also has a view of the skyline, not as impressive as the one the living room proudly boasts, but I think you'll enjoy the view it provides, nonetheless."

We move into the dining room, and while I do admire the view that it offers, it's the coffered ceiling and shadow box trim along the walls that really capture my attention.

Jasmine loved coffered ceilings. In her dream home, she often stated they were a requirement. My heart aches as her face fills my thoughts.

Maybe coming back to Georgia wasn't such a good idea.

"I just need your signature on the last page," Briana says, placing the rental agreement on the dining room table with a gold pen next to it.

I pick up the writing implement, flip quickly to the last page, and scribble my name on it.

"You know, Ms. Jamerson, you look so familiar to me. I used to read books by Raine Reynolds. I swear the two of you could be twins," she says as I lay the gold pen down.

I let out a long sigh. "Reynolds was once my last name, but I go by my maiden name now. But I'm sure you already knew that."

She gives me a half smile as she picks up the rental agreement, and then slides it inside her purse, leaving the pretty pen.

Is the pen for me? Some sort of gift or something? Part of the deal?

"You got me. Yes, I knew that. Your former last name came up when we did the background and credit check. At first, I didn't believe it was you, but when we received a copy of your driver's license, the photo confirmed it for me."

"I'm sure," I say, while trying to hide my annoyance.

"I know you probably don't do this anymore, but do you mind signing my book? It's the last one you wrote."

Now I know why she didn't pick up her gold pen.

It takes all I have not to grit my teeth as I pick up the pen, watching as she quickly pulls the book out of her purse.

"You know, I have every book you ever wrote. My mother and I loved reading them and so did our book club. I so wish you'd start writing again."

I sign her book and then hand her the pen. "That's not my life anymore."

She clearly wants to ask me why that's the case, but she doesn't.

She places the book and the gold pen back inside her purse, then pulls out a set of keys. "Well, I guess I'll let you enjoy your new home. Feel free to reach out if you need anything or if you decide to purchase the property. Again, the owner is eager to sell it."

Yes, I heard it the first time. It's still a no.

I reach out and take the keys from her. "I'll let you know if I change my mind."

She claps her hands together again. “Great. I really hope that you do.”

As we walk down the hallway, toward the foyer and front door, I can’t help but wonder if she was referring to me changing my mind about buying the place or writing again.

For me, neither is on the agenda. I promised that I would move here for a year only. In my opinion, that’s more than enough time to get the creative development and design department up and running properly. When my year is up, back to Paris is where I’ll be heading.

In fact, I already have the ticket purchased.

Chapter Twenty-Six

"ANOTHER RAINY DAY IN Georgia," the food delivery guy says as I hand him enough money to cover my food and his tip.

He counts the money and extends a full smile when he realizes I gave him a ten-dollar tip. "I work just about every day so if you need anything else delivered, just call and ask for Wan."

I nod, and then grab my food.

As I close the massive door, the scent of chicken fried rice and egg rolls fills up the foyer. I reach in the bag and pull out one of the egg rolls. It's hot, but I don't care, biting into it as I make my way down the hallway toward the living room.

Right now, I'm comfortable in a pair of shorts, a green T-shirt, and white socks.

Back in the day, I would have worn my black cotton pajamas. The ones with the pockets.

If Jasmine were here, she'd say she doesn't recognize the woman I am today. A woman who hasn't visited a bookstore in five years or written a sentence not tied to an advertising campaign somehow. She definitely would wonder why I'm sporting black, not brown, mid-back length hair that stays flat ironed on a weekly basis so that it doesn't revert to its natural curly state.

The old me would never have allowed my hair to be flat ironed or permed. My thick curls were given to me by my mother.

My eyes are still blue thanks to my father, but I thought heavily about getting hazel brown contacts while in Paris.

The day I got on the plane to Paris, that's when I left everything about my old self behind.

The tears, the pain, being an author.

A wife of a cheating husband.

A best friend to the one person I could always count on until she left me too.

Everything.

I stepped onto the cobblestone streets of Paris with nothing but the clothes on my back, shedding the memories of who I once was like pieces of old clothing. To symbolize the clarity that I finally felt, I walked into a clothing store, buying clothes that the old me would never wear.

Things with pink in them.

I almost purchased a few satin tops, but since James was the one who'd bought me the only satin top I'd owned, that idea had to be ditched.

The ad agency that I work for now was happy to take me on, being the parent company of the agency I'd worked for after college.

My old boss called in a favor for his so-called "Ace." The fact that he could include *New York Times bestselling author* while praising my credentials helped.

I didn't need the job for financial reasons, more for a sense of sanity and to help with the lonely nights that would come.

From the beginning, I dove into my work, allowing it to own every part of me, my version of crazy paid off. Each year, I rose through the ranks until I was offered a position as senior vice president of creative development and design. The only caveat was that I'd to agree to move back to Georgia, which I turned down at first because they wanted three years.

Those that I worked with thought I was crazy for saying no. But they didn't know the pain buried deep within my bones.

When I got the call that they would agree to a year, I tried to tell myself that I could handle things for that length of time.

But not a day or second more.

Maybe I was wrong about that.

My small box of chicken fried rice is half empty, both of my egg rolls gone.

I place my beer on the small glass table, staring into a sea of black cloth covering the sky, happy that the rain has finally subsided.

The clock on the wall reminds me that it's 1 a.m. and that my body is tired, but my eyes can't seem to forget that it's 7 a.m. on a Saturday morning in Paris. If I were home, I'd be sitting on my balcony, allowing the fresh morning breeze to flow through me and watching the streets come alive with local Parisians.

I close my eyes and can almost smell the bread being baked at the family-owned delicatessen near the two-bedroom villa I own in the Mouzaïa district, known for its flowered streets.

I lied to Briana. I also have a small garden. Who doesn't in Paris? And I adore it; and, yes, I still drink coffee. I'm unsure why

I denied that when Café Parisien, at the end of Danube Metro, was my daily go-to.

I glance at the clock again and sigh.

It hasn't been twenty-four hours yet, and I already miss Paris.

On Sunday mornings, I'd walk about ten minutes to the Parc des Buttes Chaumont, an amazing park in the 19th arrondissement designed by Baron Haussmann and Napoleon III.

I would stroll across the bridge there to look down into the lake and take in the freedom of the life that lived in it or venture into one of the theaters to watch a puppet show.

My favorite place, of course, was the Buttes-Chaumont Garden, one of the largest in Paris. From there, one could get an amazing view of the Montmartre district.

If you didn't feel rejuvenated there, you needed to check to make sure you had a pulse.

On my way home, I would sometimes stop at the Cent Quatre to browse the art, some a little too edgy for my taste, but just being there made me feel surrounded by inspiration.

Many of my most popular ad campaigns were written and designed because of that place.

In Paris, I was Raine Jamerson. And that was it.

And for me, that was more than enough.

Chapter Twenty-Seven

AN UNFAMILIAR CEILING LOOKS down on me the moment my eyes open. Streams of sunlight come in through the bay windows, welcoming me like a mother greeting her daughter.

I roll myself off the sofa, giving my body a good stretch.

There is mess just about everywhere from last night. *Better clean up before the whole place starts to smell like fried rice gone bad.* So, I grab my cell phone, then make my way into the kitchen to hunt for a trash bag.

Now that my body has rested, I fully take in the kitchen.

Briana, although twenty-three, thought of everything. The cabinets are filled with everything a real chef would need in a kitchen such as this. I open the refrigerator to find it fully stocked as well. There's even a box of croissants on the shelf with a sticky note attached.

I pull off the note and read it.

```
These aren't from Paris, but I think you'll
find the bakery around the corner comes close.
-Briana C.
```

Placing the note on the counter, I sigh, hating that I gave her such a hard time yesterday. From the garden on the rooftop to the mention of coffee shops and restaurants within walking distance, it's obvious that she did her research.

It will never make me give up living in Paris, but I at least need to send her a thank you card.

I grab a croissant out of the box and take a bite.

She is right. The croissants are amazing. Soft, buttery, and flaky. I can only imagine how they taste when they've just come out of the oven.

I know I'll be visiting that bakery soon.

Coffee made, it's so typical that my cellphone rings just at the moment of wanting to ease up and relax. Briana's name appears on screen just as my drink reaches my lips.

Busted.

"Morning," she says in her usual chipper voice. "I was just calling to check on you. I know the first night in a new place can be rough."

Now there's even more guilt for giving her a hard time yesterday. "Thanks. I finally got to sleep at about 1 a.m. I was surprised I slept up until 10. That's not like me."

She chuckles. "Bet you slept on the sofa."

I smile. *She's good,* I think as I switch hands with the mug. "I did, right after eating a half-container of chicken fried rice and a couple of egg rolls."

"Did you have your coffee yet?"

Now I laugh. "Okay, you got me. I made a cup to go with my croissant. Thanks, by the way, for that, and thanks for everything. You've really thought of every little thing. I'm so sorry about yesterday. I was short with you most of the evening."

"Don't worry about that. Yesterday was a long day for you, and you were tired. I was surprised you even agreed to meet me yesterday instead of this morning. Plus, I'm sure it wasn't easy leaving Paris and coming back to Georgia. I'm sure you had a reason for going to live there in the first place, and that reason was staring you in the face the moment you hit that Georgia red clay."

I lean up against the counter. "You can't be twenty-three."

She belts out a strong laugh. "I'm thirty-eight. I was messing with you when I made that comment about looking as fit as you when I get to your age. But in all fairness, you do look great. I'd love to look like you and not have to kill myself on the treadmill every day."

"Thought I heard you claim it gives you focus," I say with a bit of humor in my voice.

"Good comeback. Love it."

"You're hilarious."

"Girl, in this business, you *have to* have a sense of humor. Last night, I didn't think you had one. I guess we both made a few wrong assumptions."

I nod my head in agreement. "Sad, but true. I'm so sorry."

"Don't worry about it. One thing I've learned is that women judge each other way too quickly and all the time. Men don't. I'm just as guilty as you are."

"I'm glad you called this morning. I was going to send you a thank you card."

"The up-front commission from your one-year lease was thank you enough. I'm sure my mortgage company thanks you for contributing to my fifteen-year commitment to them."

"You should do stand-up."

"My brother says that all the time. He's the serious one, but he has his fun moments. Not as much as I believe he should, but he tries. I keep telling him that he needs a life and a girlfriend.

"Speaking of which, I know you just got back, but I'd love to have you meet him. Not a matchmaker sort of thing, just a hello so you get to meet another person in the area."

"I haven't socialized with any guy I didn't work with in five years."

"I find that hard to believe. What the heck did you do in Paris?"

"I told you, worked my butt off."

"No, what you told me is that working kept you distracted. That only means that you were running from something, and work helped you to not think about it."

Silence.

"Sorry, I know I can be direct. Once the real estate gloves come off, I get to be my true self."

"It's cool. I used to have a friend like that. It's probably why she and I got along so well."

"She passed away, huh?"

"How did you know that?"

"You said that you *used* to have a friend."

"You're a good listener. I see why you do so well in the real estate business. You could have been a shrink though! But it probably doesn't pay quite as well!"

"A trait I got, honestly. Sometimes it's good and sometimes, I need to learn to keep my mouth shut. At least, that's what my dear mother says."

"Oh, my goodness, I haven't laughed this hard in a long time," I say, hand jittering with my mug in it. "Good thing these floors are waterproof. I spilled a good amount just now on the kitchen floor."

"Hey, you can use that hot water button to get it up."

I roar with laughter. "Stop."

"I'll try. So, can you meet up tomorrow? I'll bring my brother. I promise no pressure. If you think he's too uptight like I do, I'll send him back to the closet he keeps himself locked up in, and you and I will carry on a girly chat."

"I'm not looking to date anyone."

"Neither is he," she assures me. Or she tries. "So, both of you will be on the same page. I just need to get him out of the house. He's like you, all he does is work."

"Right. Well, what kind of work does he do?"

I hear a click. "Raine, sorry, that's a client calling. See you tomorrow at noon?"

"Okay."

I place my phone on the counter and stare at the sticky floor.

What have I done?

Chapter Twenty-Eight

A FLUTTER OF SUNLIGHT flows into my room. For a second, I forget I'm not in my own bed.

I throw the cover off me and then sit up, resting my head against the gray upholstered headboard. In the corner of the bedroom, empty suitcases sit next to the dresser.

The rest of my luggage finally arrived yesterday afternoon, and the car leasing company called last night to tell me the car would be delivered early Tuesday instead of tomorrow. I was okay with that, not scheduled to go into the new office until Wednesday.

My phone dings, and I look over to see a text from Briana.

Please say you're canceling today.

But no. She's not.

> Happy Sunday! Like you, it took some extra convincing, but my brother is up for meeting you. See you at noon. Don't dare cancel.

```
I know where you live. Smiley
face. No pressure, though.
```

Her brother is up for meeting me? So, it has definitely been put across as a date. Sounds as if she's twisting his arm or something. *Ugh.*

Pressure is all I'm feeling right now, and yes, I do want to cancel.

Why did I agree to this foolishness?

I check the time before placing my phone back down on the nightstand, surprised to find I've slept until nine. Even on the weekends back home in Paris, I never slept past 7 a.m. But I feel good, well rested, so maybe it's not such a bad thing. *Am I more comfortable here than I realize?*

I push down on the mattress and make a mental note to order the same brand when I get back home.

My phone dings again.

```
Sorry, forgot to send you the address
of Morning Run, the coffee shop we're
meeting at today. It's just around
the corner. Look for the dog park.
```

I start texting a reply.

```
Hi, sorry, but I'm not going to make it.
```

My finger rests on the send button.

I delete my text.

`Okay. I'll see you there.`

A long sigh escapes as I put the phone down again and head to the shower.

Chapter Twenty-Nine

WALKING INTO THE COFFEE show, I spot Briana sitting at a table. Alone.

He didn't come. I could have kept that old T-shirt on.

As I make my way over to Briana, I can't help but take in the smells and sounds of chatter filling the space between the walls and tables, listening to the hum of coffee machines, the grinding of beans and tapping of fingers on laptops, spoons stirring in cream or milk.

I feel my shoulders drop.

"Hey, girl. Love that floral dress!" Briana says. "I have the perfect pair of yellow sandals that would match it. I'm a huge fan of all things yellow. Summery."

"I don't think I own a pair of yellow sandals," I say, pulling a chair out and then taking a seat.

"I would say you could borrow mine, but if you're like me, you wouldn't dare put your feet in another woman's shoes."

A small chuckle escapes me. "You really should do stand-up."

"Who has time for that foolishness?" she asks.

"Trust me when I say that you need to make time. You'd be great."

"Maybe one day, I'll be brave enough to take this show on the road. My house needs to be paid for first. We can't all pay cash for our residences, can we? But I suspect, any six-time New York Times bestselling author can." She smiles and then takes a sip of her drink.

"I didn't—"

Her eyebrows rise. "You know I'm a real estate agent, right? One search on the address from your license and…"

"Okay. I paid cash for my villa."

"Nice. Not only do I need your body when I turn forty, I also need to be in your financial position when I hit that age. I'm almost there."

I blink with surprise. "Wow. That's great."

"A lot of hard work. I'd probably already be there if I left the stores alone. Shoes, especially."

I shrug a bit. "I wouldn't know. Haven't been shopping in five years."

"So let me guess, the moment you got to Paris, you went on a shopping spree. Am I right?"

I stare at her.

"It's what we women do when we feel like we need to start over."

"Like I said, you should be a shrink."

She takes a sip of her drink. "That's my brother's area of expertise, not mine. Speaking of which, here he is."

I turn around and see Donovan walking in.

"Donovan," I clumsily say as he walks to our table.

"Raine Reynolds."

"Jamerson," I say too quickly.

"Right."

Briana stands up and hugs him. "I was beginning to think you were going to stand us up."

"I ran into traffic due to the bike race." His eyes stay on me as I reach down and adjust my dress, although I know it doesn't need it.

Briana takes a step back and stares at both of us. "I didn't know you two had met before."

My eyes plead for him not to mention that I'd been a patient.

"It was years ago, and very briefly."

My shoulders relax some.

"Nice. Well, give her a hug since you're long-lost friends."

He sneers at Briana, who acts as if she could care less, but then reaches over and gives me a hug.

He's changed his cologne. Smells even better! Glad I wore the floral dress.

"How have you been? It's been some time."

He keeps his face straight, giving nothing away.

"Living in Paris."

"Nice."

"Have you ever been?"

Briana jumps in before he can respond. "My brother has never left the state of Georgia. He lives and breathes his work. So do I, but I still know how to get out and have fun."

I can't help but laugh. "Well, if that's the case, it's nice you're so committed to your work."

"That's nice of you to say."

"It sure is," Briana says with a smirk. "But so not true. I keep telling him that he needs to get out and come do stuff with me."

He looks over at her. "I'm here, aren't I? What more do you want?"

Briana smirks again. "You win that one."

"Shall we end the battle, just for today?"

She nods in agreement. "I'm glad you came."

His smile softens, the cute dimple settling into his cheek.

"Have you gotten your coffee yet?" he asks.

Briana's phone rings just as I'm about to say no. "Sorry, I need to take this. Why don't you two grab your coffees and I'll step outside."

We both turn and look at the long line that has formed.

"It just looks long. Go ahead. I'll be a few minutes anyway."

We walk to the back of the line as she steps outside to take her call.

"You look nice, by the way."

I nervously pull my hair behind my ear. "Thanks."

What is it with this man that has me blushing like a schoolgirl?

"How long have you been back in Georgia?"

"Your sister didn't tell you? Got in Friday night."

"Actually, my sister didn't mention that anyone else was going to be joining us. She just told me that I had to come because it was important, and if I didn't, she wouldn't speak to me for a year."

"So, you could have gone a full year of your sister not trying to fix you up, and you didn't take it?"

A soft chuckle escapes his lips, and I can't help but notice the strong lines of his jaw.

Were those there before?

"I know my sister. She would have stayed mad at me for about a month, tops."

I look over at Briana and she waves.

"So, how do you know my sister?"

"She helped me find the place that I'm leasing."

"That makes sense."

"It's just around the corner," I add.

Girl, the man didn't ask where you live.

"This is a great area. You couldn't have chosen better."

"That's what she said. It's close to my job. I'm here to help get my company's creative development and design team up and running."

"So, you're not writing anymore?"

"I didn't realize that you knew I was an author."

"Ruthie recognized you. She mentioned it after you left that day."

"Not your kind of books, I take it?"

"Women's fiction normally isn't, but they are good. Ruthie insisted I read a few of them. She knows how much I love books. And I'm glad I did."

"I remember seeing shelves full of books. You have quite the collection."

"Not all were medical books, by the way."

"Of course not. At least one or two are mine."

He issues a gentle laugh.

Okay, he laughs.

He looks over at his sister. "I bet she's not really talking to anyone."

I look over in her direction. "She looks like she is."

"I'm sure she's pretending."

"I hope not. It's pretty hot and humid out there."

"She'd say it was worth it." He looks at me. "And I'd agree with her."

Goodness. Is he flirting with me?

Don't blush.

I look up at him, and our eyes say hello as if it's the first time they've met.

I'm blushing. Like full-on cheek-to-cheek blushing.

"So, what are you going to order?" he asks.

"I think I'll try one of those French vanilla lattes."

"Feeling homesick?"

We both laugh.

So, he does have a sense of humor.

Chapter Thirty

I KEEP WAITING FOR that feeling of uneasiness to creep in as I sit here engaging in a conversation that moves from top television shows to favorite ice cream flavors. But there is none.

I catch Donovan glancing over at me a few times; is he looking at me as a client or as a woman?

Because let's face it, I'm stealing peeks of him as well, and it's not as my therapist.

There's something about him, something I can't put my finger on. When we met five years ago, he seemed so sure of himself. Not in an arrogant way. Well, maybe a little. But now, I look at him just as a man sitting across from me in a light blue shirt that pairs well with his ebony skin tone and a pair of dark denim jeans.

I don't see that trace of standoffishness that once lingered around the corners of his eyes. What I see now is how softness frames his face, and I wonder what changed.

Briana picks up her phone and taps on it. "Sorry guys, I don't want to disrupt the flow of this amazing conversation the three of us are having, but I just got a text from a client I need to meet." She stands up and grabs her empty cup.

"Put that purse down," she says as I grab my purse to leave. "The two of you don't need to leave just because I need to run. Stay. The next latte's on me."

"I can't drink another latte, and it's getting late."

"It's two o'clock, and the sun is shining. Why don't the two of you go for a walk? There's a nice little park about two blocks or so from here." She looks down at my shoes. "You've got flats on, so a nice walk to the park is perfect. Don't you think, Donovan?"

"Raine is right; it's late."

"You two act like old people." She leans over the table and stares Donovan in the eyes. "I'm sure you could use the walk and the sunshine as well."

He looks over at me. We both know she isn't going to give up on this.

"I'll go for a walk with you if you're up to it."

"I can walk," I say, kicking myself for giving such a simple response.

Briana stands back up. "Perfect."

She stuffs her phone in her purse and then leans over to hug me. "I can tell he likes you," she whispers before letting me go. "All right, I'm off to show a property and make enough money to pay my mortgage off." She gives me a wink. "You two have an amazing time at the park." She hugs her brother, and when he smiles, I know she's whispered something similar in his ear.

Chapter Thirty-One

FINDING A BENCH UNDERNEATH a weeping willow tree at the park, we take a seat and watch as a stream of bikers passes us by.

A soft breeze lingers around us, and I find myself enjoying how the breeze causes the leaves of the willow tree to move so freely that I can't help but want to feel more of that in my life.

"I've always wanted to be a part of one of those bike races."

"I've never ridden a bike in my life," I say. "It's not because I had some traumatic childhood or anything. No Mommy or Daddy issues either."

He eyes me with a concerned look. "I'm messing with you, Dr. Carter," I say.

He leans back into the bench. "You're not the first person to make that 'Mommy, Daddy' joke."

"I'm sure you get that a lot when people find out you're a shrink, I mean, therapist."

His eyes look out into the crowd of people standing along the park's curves, watching the bikers go by. "I let my practice go some years ago. I'm a professor at Emory University now, teaching psychology. My sister thinks I treat my students like my patients. That I'm too vested."

I try to hide my stunned look. "Why the change?"

"It was always something I considered doing, so when the opportunity presented itself, I took it. The time was right."

"How did Ruthie take that news?"

"It wasn't an easy conversation, but she understood since I was selling the house anyway."

"I guess I'll never get a tour of that house now." His eyebrows raise slightly. "Ruthie promised that she'd give me a tour after my second session. I'm still not sure why it had to be after that. But it was something she'd offered."

He sits back up. "She always told patients that; it gave them two reasons to come back."

I chuckle some. "She's something else. Do you two keep in touch?"

"Ruthie passed away from cancer about six months after your visit."

I place my hand over my mouth. "She didn't look like she was sick," I finally say.

"She hid it well, didn't want treatment or pity and often said that she preferred to live her life enjoying all the little things." His eyes soften, and he looks off into the distance to stare for a long moment before continuing. "Ruthie once told me that nothing she did could stop the cancer growing, but once a flower was in her hands, it had no choice but to grow."

"I can tell that you miss her very much and she meant a lot to you."

"I do miss her. We worked together for years. I never considered myself her boss. To me, Ruthie was like a favorite aunt. She always thought I was the smart one. In her eyes, I could help anyone overcome anything, but what she didn't know is that she was *my* shrink."

He winks at me, and I smile, but looking out at the crowd again, I think about Ruthie, and then about my mother and how much I miss her.

"My mother died from cancer when I was young. It was just my father and me for a long time. Then, he was killed in car accident while taking me to the hospital."

I was expecting him to say something *shrink-like*, but he reaches over and takes my hand into his own. "So, you do have Mommy, Daddy issues."

I belt out a laugh so loud a few people turn to stare at us.

Chapter Thirty-Two

MY STOMACH GROWLS. ALL I had for lunch was a venti-sized French vanilla latte.

Donovan looks over at me and grins. "Sounds like you could eat."

Oh goodness, he heard it.

Embarrassed, I place my hand on my stomach, but it growls again.

"Okay, let's go and get you something. My sister would never forgive me if I told her I left you with a grumbly stomach."

"This is so embarrassing."

He stands up and reaches out his hand.

Our eyes dance together under the weeping willow tree as I place my hand in his, and then stand. "What do you recommend?"

His eyebrows furrow. "Do you like Chinese food?"

"I've never met an egg roll that I didn't like."

He chuckles and then gently intertwines his fingers into mine. "I feel the same way about egg drop soup."

Are we holding hands? I glance down for a second.

Am I okay with this?

He smiles and his dimple returns.

Yes. I'm okay with it.

"I've never had egg drop soup."

"I'll have to make you some."

I stop and face him. "Wait, you know how to make egg drop soup?"

"*And* egg rolls."

I study his face, trying to figure out if he's kidding. "Are you serious?"

"Do you want to find out?"

"You mean like right now?"

"Sure. Why not? There's a great Asian market not too far from here. We could head back to the coffee shop, grab my car, and then make a quick market run so I can grab the things that I need. I hope you're okay with dark meat chicken because I make mine with it."

"I'm okay with anything that I don't have to cook!"

He grins. I continue, "You're going to have to tell me how you know how to make egg rolls." We make our way back.

"My mother learned how to make them when she was in culinary school, and she taught Briana and me how to make them and egg drop soup."

"The condo I'm leasing has a kitchen that would love you."

"In that case, let's pick up everything from the market and head back to your place."

"Sounds good to me."

Now I understand why Briana felt the kitchen was the most important space in a home.

Chapter Thirty-Three

WALKING INTO MY PLACE with Donovan right behind me with a handful of grocery bags excites me, but a slight hint of unsureness creeps up on me as I show him to the kitchen.

He places the bags down on the counter, then looks around. "Yes, I would love to have a kitchen like this. After selling the house, I opted for a four-bedroom townhome. It's one of those three level units. It has a decent kitchen, but nothing like this. I'm going to get my sister for not showing this place to me."

I look around again.

"The kitchen in my villa in Paris is half this size. I don't cook much, so I don't need a large kitchen, but you're right, this one's massive and extremely nice, definitely built for a chef.

"Briana mentioned that the seller of this place is eager to sell it. My lease is up in a year, so maybe you can put in an offer!"

"Oh, so you're only here for a year."

The concerned look on his face is genuine this time.

"My company would like me to stay for three years."

His shoulders relax. "Well, I hope they convince you to stay. I know I'm going to do my part."

Don't blush again.

Too late. The heat in my cheeks is betraying me.

The groceries are still sitting untouched. "Are you ready to prove to me that you can make egg rolls?"

"Do you have a couple of aprons?"

"We only need one. *I'm* not cooking!"

He gives me a sly smile. "My mother always says that the more hands there are in the kitchen, the faster one eats. I do remember someone's stomach growling just a while ago."

"Okay. I'll do what I can, but I did warn you I'm no chef."

"I know people who call themselves chefs but can't cook, and I know people who can cook but would never call themselves chefs."

"Which one are you?" I ask with a wink.

"Let's find out together."

I lean against the counter and watch as he pulls out a pack of frozen egg roll wrappers from one of the grocery bags. "We'll let these thaw at room temperature. It should only take about forty-five minutes or so."

Forty-five minutes? I pray my stomach doesn't start growling again.

He begins opening each kitchen drawer.

"What are you looking for?"

"Found them. Here you go," he says, tossing an apron at me.

Briana, this is your fault!

"What do you want to do first?" I ask, with as much displeasure in my tone as I can muster.

"You look cute when you pout, but cuteness isn't going to get you out of this. Why don't you start by placing the vermicelli rice noodles in a bowl and then filling the bowl with very hot water. Once that's done, take two forks and begin to separate the noodles."

Well, I guess that hot water button is going to come in handy again. "What does the hot water do?" I ask, as I cover the rice noodles completely with hot water and then grab two forks out of the drawer.

"After separating the noodles, you'll let them sit in the hot water for about five to seven minutes to let them get tender."

I start gently separating the rice noodles. "Am I doing this right?" He places the cabbage in his hands down and comes up behind me. "You do it like this." He places his hands on top of mine, and we begin to separate the noodles together.

His breath lingers on my neck as he talks about the importance of using the forks to keep them from sticking.

"There," he says, "that should do it. Let's place them aside."

"For seven minutes, right?"

"More or less," he says, stepping away and returning to the lettuce. "After that, you'll want to drain them in a colander. Be sure to drain them very well and then rinse them with cold water to keep them from sticking. The cold water helps stop the cooking process. The last step is to chop them up into about 1-inch pieces. Hopefully, there's a cutting board somewhere in one of the cabinets."

I open the cabinets until I find a cutting board, then give it a quick rinse off. "Do they stay in the cold water?"

"No, we'll place them in a mixing bowl."

"Okay, let me find that as well."

He begins to slice up about four cups of green cabbage. "You're pretty fast."

He grins. "I've done this a few times, but the trick is to use a serrated knife. It helps create thin slices and doesn't stick to the cabbage during slicing." He places the knife down on the counter. "You want to give it a try?"

"Sure."

Once again, he places a hand on top of mine and guides me as I slice the cabbage. "I can't believe how easy this is," I say as his cologne fills the air and me.

"You're a natural."

"Okay, what's next?"

He grins again. "I knew you would enjoy this."

The cooking or you?

"Grab those brown mushrooms over on the counter, rinse them in water, then pat them dry. Once you're done, I'll slice them up. They have to be pretty thin."

"Yes, Chef."

"Funny." He looks over at the rice noodles. "They should be ready to drain now."

I start working on the noodles again while he slices up the mushrooms.

I could... No girl, you've had enough cologne moments for the day.

"When I'm done with these, do you want me to grate the carrots, or is there something special that needs to be done to them?"

"I saw a Julienne slicer in the drawer. You'll use that to cut the carrots into matchsticks."

"That sounds fancy," I say, retrieving the slicer.

"I'll work on finely chopping a medium onion after these mushrooms, and that will be all that's needed for the prep work."

"I'm all done," I say, taking off my apron after finishing up the carrots.

"Oh no, you don't. Put that apron back on."

"I thought you said that was all the prep work."

"It is, but now we move to the next steps."

I place my apron back on reluctantly.

"We're almost there, I promise."

"I hope so. If not, you're going to hear my stomach start to growl again."

"If you look in one of the grocery bags, you'll find a small bowl of fruit."

"Nice," I say, rushing over to find the fruit. "This will tide me over."

He watches me for a second as I quickly devour a couple of pieces.

"Sorry. I'm so hungry. You want some?"

He shakes his head. "No, you go ahead and enjoy that." He looks under the cabinet and grabs a skillet. "This is a nice skillet."

"You'll have to thank your sister for that. She thought of everything."

"I see. I wonder why I didn't get that kind of treatment when she sold me my townhome."

"Did she get full commission?"

He smiles. "Good point. She did give me the 'brother discount.'"

"Also, remember that I requested a fully furnished condo."

"This one is definitely fully furnished." He places the skillet on the stove and then grabs some olive oil and a container of shredded chicken out of a grocery bag. "I'll get started on sautéing the shredded chicken in a little bit of this olive oil."

"I would have never thought to buy chicken already shredded."

"I usually make my own. Once I'm finishing sautéing the chicken, I'll add it to the noodles in the mixing bowl and then come back and sauté the mushrooms, carrots, and onions together. Once the mushrooms, carrots, and onions are nice and tender, I'll add our shredded cabbage, toss everything together and let it cook until the cabbage looks wilted, mix in about a half-teaspoon of salt, take it off the heat, and then transfer it to the mixing bowl with the chicken and noodles.

"Now I just need to add another half-teaspoon of salt, a half-teaspoon of black pepper, two tablespoons of soy sauce, and then one teaspoon of sesame oil."

"Do you start building the eggs rolls after that?"

"*We* will." He gives me a wink as I stuff a few more pieces of fruit in my mouth and then watch him start to mix everything together.

"Man, it smells and looks amazing. Can you use meat other than shredded dark meat chicken for the egg rolls?"

"Sure."

"Really? Like what?"

"Briana likes to use pork."

"You don't eat pork, I take it."

"It's sort of like reading women's fiction for me."

I pick out a piece of melon and throw it at him.

"Hey, you're not supposed to abuse the chef."

"Sorry, Chef."

He picks up a couple pieces of a mushroom and tosses them at me. "As they say… all's fair in eggs rolls and cooking."

"Who says that?"

He shrugs his shoulders, and we fill the kitchen with a bit of laughter.

Chapter Thirty-Four

"OKAY, CHEF, WHAT ARE we doing now?" I ask after tossing the empty fruit bowl into the trash and then washing my hands.

"You really like calling me that, don't you?"

"It's better than calling you a shrink."

"I like that you have a good sense of humor."

"The way your sister described you, I almost didn't think you had one."

He stops what he's doing and leans up against the counter so that we face each other.

"Years ago, I took life way too seriously. Don't get me wrong, I still take things seriously, but I've tried adding other aspects into my personality. I can tell my students enjoy humor. Psychology can be boring if you don't laugh."

"I get that. I like this version of you."

His eyes brighten. "Do you really?"

He steps over to me and places his hands on my waist. Our eyes block out everything except each other. "When I first saw you in that Waffle House, I thought you were very pretty, but I could see that James was into you and that you were into him. You didn't even look my way. Was it because I was too serious even back then?"

I purse my lips and narrow my eyes. "So, you did remember me from that day?"

"Of course. When I saw you at my old house, you were a little older, as was I, but I knew it was you the moment I walked in to do the session."

"That session with you really helped. More than you know, but the evening before my next session with you, I got a call that my best friend had been killed."

I see a sadness in his eyes, knowing he's thinking about Ruthie. We've both lost someone important to us.

"I'm sorry for your loss," he says.

Those are words that people say in situations like this, but when they fall from his lips, I appreciate them. We've both lost someone we loved and cared about.

"I am too," I say. "There's not a day that goes by that I don't miss her. After her funeral, I left immediately. Twelve hours later, I arrived in Paris with nothing but the clothes on my back.

"Paris became my savior in a sense."

"Are you saying that you found yourself in Paris?"

"You sound like your sister."

"I've watched that movie *Sabrina* with her and my mother a million times."

"You're a good brother."

"I'd like to be a better boyfriend."

"Would you now?"

He leans in and gently places his lips on mine. "Absolutely."

The doctor is smooth. Who knew?

"You ready to get started putting the egg rolls together?"

"Sure," I say as he steps back over to the egg roll mixture. "I'm going to drain this to remove any excess moisture from the mixture. If you'll grab the peanut oil from the bag, I think I saw one of those Dutch ovens in that tall cabinet next to the pantry. We'll get to rolling."

"Rolling egg rolls sounds so exciting," I say sarcastically as he finishes draining off the mixture and then grabs the now thawed egg roll wrappers.

"After we've rolled all forty, I know you'll think so."

"Did you say forty? I doubt the two of us can eat forty egg rolls."

"I'm sure we can't. I'll take what's left and drop them off at a shelter I know of, but some of them can be frozen."

"That sounds great. What about the egg drop soup you're supposed to be making?"

"I didn't forget. Prepping the soup takes about five minutes and one pot. It only takes ten minutes to cook, so I'll be working on that while you're frying up the last two batches of egg rolls."

"I can't wait to try it."

He grabs some paper towels and then dampens them, placing them over the egg roll wrappers.

"Is that to keep them from drying out?"

"It is. Can you beat an egg for me and see if you can find a small pastry brush?"

"For the soup?" I ask as I open the drawer, then pull out a small brush.

"That's perfect. The egg is for sealing the egg rolls. We'll add a bit of it on the last flap of our egg roll."

"Is this going to be like rolling croissants? You start at one end of a triangle and roll, keeping it tight?"

"Very similar. Here, I'll show you." He peels back one layer of an egg roll wrapper and then replaces the damp paper towel on the rest. "If I were at home, I would use a much bigger wooden cutting board, but the one here works. Like you mentioned, I do lay the egg roll wrapper in a triangle, then using a one-fourth-cup measure, I add my mixture to the bottom third of the wrapper and then pull the corner over the mixture. Like this."

I peek over to get a good look at what he's doing.

"You smell nice. I meant to tell you that before," he says.

"Oh, you mean when you were leaning over to kiss me."

"What kind of perfume is that?" He pulls me to him and then wraps his arms around my waist, bringing us even closer together. "You know you didn't answer my question," he whispers.

"What question was that?"

"The one about being your boyfriend."

"I thought you were making more of a statement than a question."

"So, you're saying that I need to ask properly? Do they do that now?"

"I'm saying you have forty egg rolls to wrap."

He pulls slowly away. "You're right, we do, but I'm not giving up on getting a response to my *statement*."

"I'm glad we agree that it was a statement," I say as he moves back to the counter. He tucks his egg roll wrapper under the mixture and begins to roll it, making sure to keep it tight as he rolls while folding in the corners. When he's about a quarter of the way done, he uses some of the egg to brush the edges and then rolls the rest of it. "Pretty easy, isn't it?"

"Like you said, after rolling forty of those bad babies, I think I'll get the hang of it."

"I don't know the name of your perfume, but it reminds me of a garden. Maybe we should do this…"

I cut him off. "Just keep rolling there, Chef." He gives me a sly smile as I grab another cutting board and start on my egg roll. He stops for a minute, pulling a sheet of plastic wrap off the roller to place on top of the egg rolls that we've completed.

"Do you mind if I ask you a question about your writing?"

"I don't."

"Was the death of your friend the reason you stopped?"

I place my hands down on the counter for a second. "She was also my publicist. After she died, I just couldn't find the inspiration anymore."

"Paris didn't help?"

"I got a job back in the ad business. It's what I did before I started writing. My work kept me so busy I didn't have time to think about penning novels."

"How did your publishing company take that news?"

"They weren't happy to say the least. But thankfully, I'd just written a book that fulfilled my contract with them. They tried hard to get me to renew."

"Do you think you'll ever write again?"

"There were moments when an idea would pop into my head for a story, but my work on the ad campaigns I was managing quickly clouded out those moments. Leaving not a spare minute to myself."

"I'm sure your fans would love to read another book from you."

"Your sister certainly would love that. You know she talked me into signing a copy of the last book I wrote for her."

"That sounds like Briana. Did she use her gold pen?"

I nod. "You know she did. What's the story with that pen?"

"When she became a real estate agent, she purchased it. Every time a client signed a contract with her, she would make sure they used that pen. The pen represented her promise."

"Promise to do what?"

"To give each and every client, no matter how big she got, the same level of what she called 'gold-level' service."

I look around the kitchen again. "She certainly did that for me."

"Yeah, I agree. And even though she gave me the *brother* discount on the commission, she treated me like a full-commissioned client."

"I didn't realize how important that pen was."

"Ruthie used to say that it's the small things that hold more value for us."

"So true."

"I think that pen cost Briana less than a hundred dollars, but it means so much more to her."

"I like that story."

"Me too," he says, pouring the peanut oil into the Dutch oven, then grabbing a thermometer.

"This is getting serious."

"At some point, I hope that it does."

"I was referring to you getting out the thermometer."

"So was I."

I raise my eyebrows.

"I was."

"How long do we cook them?" I ask.

"About five minutes. We'll need a wire rack to put them on. That keeps them crisp."

"Good to know," I say, grabbing the thermometer from him and sticking it in the oil. "What temp should it be at?"

"About 350. You'll drop about five or six of the egg rolls at a time to ensure the temperature stays consistent. Too many in at once cause the temperature to drop quickly."

"This really is serious."

He smiles this time. "I'm not falling for that one again."

"I don't know what you're talking about, Chef."

"Oh goodness, here we go with that again. I think I'll go and get the soup going since you seem to have a good handle on the egg rolls."

"Yes, Chef."

He shakes his head.

Boyfriend?

Is this moving too fast?

You haven't said yes to anything.

Take it slow, Raine.

Learn from your mistakes.

You can't go from therapist to coffee to boyfriend. Right?

No, that's crazy. But then again, so was jumping on a plane to Paris and starting over.

My phone rings.

"Hi, it's Briana. How did the walk to the park go?"

"How did the property showing go if there really was one?"

"Of course, there was. Maybe not in the timeframe I said, but I did have one with a client today."

I smile. "I thought so."

"What are you doing?"

"Your brother and I are making egg rolls."

"Really? I love his egg rolls. In my opinion, he makes them better than our mother."

"Why don't you come over?"

"Why, do you two need a chaperone or is my brother so boring that you need me to bring the fun to your late lunch?"

I can't help but chuckle. "I'll see you when you get here."

I let out a sigh of relief, glancing over at Donovan stirring in the eggs for his soup.

I could get use to a man who cooks.

He shows me his pearly whites.

Hurry up, Briana.

Chapter Thirty-Five

"SIS, WHAT ARE YOU doing here?"

"I heard you were cooking up your famous egg rolls, so I brought a bottle of wine to go with them."

He grins, but there's disappointment behind it.

Did I mess up here?

"Why don't we go up to the rooftop?" Briana suggests.

"I have yet to see it, so that sounds great," I say.

"There's a picnic basket in the closet. We could pack everything in it. I'll go grab it."

I turn to Donovan once I'm sure Briana's out of earshot. "I should have mentioned that I invited your sister."

"No, it's okay. I get it."

"Get what?"

"Your response to my *statement*."

"Donovan…"

Before I can finish my sentence, Briana walks back into the kitchen with the picnic basket.

"Man, those egg rolls smell delicious. Bro, did you also make your egg drop soup?"

"I did. Why don't you and Raine enjoy it and the egg rolls?" He looks at this watch. "I want to make it to the shelter with some of the egg rolls before they close the kitchen."

"That shelter's in for a treat," I say, trying to get a smile from him, but he doesn't look in my direction.

Briana puts a few egg rolls in plastic bags and then adds the soup into two empty containers. "I can't wait to dig in. I'm starving."

I try again to get Donovan's attention.

"You have to be hungry as well, Donovan. Sure you don't want to join us on the roof? My car will be here on Tuesday if you give me the address. I'll be happy to drop the egg rolls off then. Stay, please," I say.

He finally looks me in the eyes and pulls off his apron. "Sure. I'll stay."

I let out a sigh of relief.

"Okay, I've got everything packed into this baby. Let's go eat," Briana says, lifting the picnic basket up.

"Let me carry that, Sis."

"I got it."

"We need glasses for the wine," I say, hoping to get a moment alone with him before we all head to the roof. "Donovan, you want to help me grab a few of them? Briana, you go ahead, Donovan and I can meet you on the roof."

"The plastic kind are usually in the basket, right, Sis?"

"They are, but we could use the real thing if Raine prefers."

He keeps his eyes on Briana. "I think those will be fine. Let's go," he says, moving out of the kitchen quickly before I can say anything else.

Yep, I'm sure I messed this up.

Chapter Thirty-Six

THE BRIGHT LIGHT OF morning hits me squarely in the face as I turn over to face the window. I hate that I forgot to close the curtains last night, and yes, I'm blaming Donovan for that.

In fact, I blame him for not sleeping well last night too. All night, I kept replaying what happened between us on the rooftop. He wasn't *un*friendly. In fact, in some ways, he was friendlier on the rooftop than at the coffee shop.

He laughed.

He smiled at everything his sister said or did.

As for me though, he barely looked my way unless I forced it. At one point in the conversation last night, I almost screamed, "Remember me, the girl you just made forty egg rolls with? The girl who invited you back to her apartment? The girl you just kissed ever so gently?"

But I didn't. Instead, I sat there telling myself not to get worked up about it. We had a moment, and obviously, it ended.

I'm leaving in a year. Maybe he figured that out. Maybe we both should. But maybe…

Maybe the moment he kissed me, I saw a door. A door that I haven't allowed myself to see in five years. Not that the door is completely unlocked, but I definitely felt the key turning.

I sit up, throw the covers off, then grab my phone off the nightstand to check my email. The first message I see is marked urgent, so I click on it and see it's from Kimberly, the assistant to all the executives. I know she's still upset that I made all my own arrangements to come here. She asked a hundred times if I needed her to book my plane tickets, trying hard to intervene and coordinate things with Briana, but in the end, I finally had to tell her that I would take care of things myself. "Things" as in everything.

I needed to do it.

No, I had to do it.

That was the only way I was going to get on a plane and come back to a place like this, one I swore never to frequent again. For over thirty years, Georgia's presence in my life had made a home. But then a wrecking ball came crashing through, my world crumbling down.

I have no regrets about leaving. *That's a lie.*

There is one regret. I regret not saying goodbye to Jasmine's parents. Vicky has called me a million times, but I hit the ignore button each time her number pops up.

Ignore.

That word sticks to me as I slowly realize that I'm not just ignoring Vicky; I've been ignoring everything, moving on from the devastation.

I lean up against the headboard and let out a long sigh, tears welling up.

This is why I never wanted to come back here.

I wipe the first tear away, and as the next one falls, place my phone back down on the nightstand and surrender to them all.

Twenty minutes pass.

Then ten more.

Finally, I wipe my face for the hundredth time and then pick my phone back up to read the email from Kimberly.

> Hi Ms. Jamerson,
>
> The building management company called and stated there's been a major water leak in the office building due to faulty sprinkler systems. The ceilings, walls, and floors were severely damaged as a result. Electricity is out, making the building unusable.
>
> Unfortunately, they are saying that it will take two weeks just to get a full assessment of what needs to be done to repair things sufficiently enough to work there.
>
> I'm happy to keep in touch with the building management company and provide you weekly updates as necessary.
>
> Best,
> Kimberly

I grab a pillow and toss it.
Is it too early in the morning to eat egg rolls?

Chapter Thirty-Seven

MY CELLPHONE PINGS WITH a text message just as I'm about to send Kimberly a reply to her email.

It's from Donovan.

> Hi, I think I left my wallet.

I walk into the kitchen and sure enough, there it is, his wallet sitting on the counter.

> Yep, I'm looking at it now. I was going to head over to the coffee shop in a few minutes. Do you want to meet me there to get it?

Three dots appear.

> Isn't it raining outside?

Are you afraid of a little rain?

I add a smiley face.

Glad you're still being friendly
after my behavior last night.

How can I not be friendly to the person
who taught me how to make egg rolls? I
have this fantastic coffee machine if
you'd prefer to just come over here.

I pause, and then hit the back button to delete the last part of my text.

How can I not be friendly to the
person who taught me how to make egg
rolls? See you in ten minutes or so.

I place my phone in my pocket, then head to my bedroom to rummage through my clothes.

So, do I wear jeans and a top that says, "let's be friends"... Or throw on another cute dress that says, "let's start over?"

I toss a couple pairs of jeans on the bed and then grab a few simple tops. My blue dress stares back at me, but I refuse to pull it off the hanger.

I hear a ping on my cell, dashing over to the dresser.

I'm here.

`Sorry, I'm heading there now, I reply.`

`Don't forget my wallet.`

Goodness. How did he know I'd forget?

I grab my purse, toss my phone inside, then run into the kitchen to grab his wallet. As I hit the foyer, I stop and glance at myself in one of the full-length mirrors.

Hope I made the right choice.

Chapter Thirty-Eight

THE COFFEE SHOP'S PACKED as I walk in, but I spot Donovan at a table in the corner.

That man knows he's handsome. That gray suit, crisp white shirt with an open button… looks good on him. And then there's the smile.

"Hi there," I say, taking a seat. "You look like a professor in that suit."

His smile spreads, and I place my hand on the table to keep myself steady.

Girl, you've always been a sucker for a good smile.

"You look great yourself. That blue dress goes well with your eyes. You must be headed to work."

No, I wore this dress for you.

"Funny thing about work. I received an email this morning that there was a water leak. So now the office won't be ready for weeks. But I'm going to go by to check on things myself."

That's partially true. I'm going to drop by. Just not today.

"I can give you a lift if you like."

"You look like you're headed to teach a class this morning. I wouldn't want to hold you up."

"The students are out for the summer, but I was going to stop by the school."

And you always wear a suit that looks like it was tailor-made, just to stop by the school?

I reach into my purse and pull out his wallet. "Before I forget. Here you go."

"Thanks," he says, and then pauses. "I want to apologize for last night."

"Yes, what was that all about?"

He reaches over, placing his hand on top of mine, the warmth of his skin melting into mine.

"I like you, Raine, and I thought we were connecting, but when you called my sister over, I took that to mean you weren't interested."

"I am interested and like you as well, but…"

"But you want to take things slow," he says, finishing my sentence. "I didn't mean to scare you off by stating that I'd make a good boyfriend."

"You have to understand, I haven't had a boyfriend in twenty years. And I'm…"

I feel his thumb making a gentle circle on my hand.

"Leaving in a year. I know."

"A year and some weeks now, it seems."

"Look, I'll take whatever time with you I can get. I'm willing to see if this can be something, and if in a year and a few weeks from now, you decide to go back to Paris, we'll cross that bridge then. Let's just see how things pan out."

"That's a mighty long bridge to cross."

"And perilous!" He winks at me, melting my heart. "But if we're on the other side of it, I'd say it was worth the journey."

Our hands fit perfectly together. Natural, even. But everything fits perfectly in the beginning. It did with James. Still, I can feel the door opening. Although slowly.

"Let's just spend some time together. We'll leave the 'boyfriend' discussion off the table *for now*," he says with yet another wink. "How does that sound to you?"

"I'll answer that question, but only after you answer a question for me first."

His eyebrows rise.

"Did you intentionally put on that suit so I could see how handsome you are in it?"

"Ms. Jamerson. Are you insinuating I made this effort for you? That's preposterous."

I raise my eyebrows.

"Well, okay, maybe… Did it work?"

"Of course not," I say, winking back.

He pulls my hand up to his lips and places a soft kiss on it. "So, are we starting over?"

"Yes, we're starting over."

Chapter Thirty-Nine

I FEEL LIKE A girl going on her first date as I slide into a pair of open-toed gold heels. Only this isn't our first date. It's our fourth in two weeks.

Donovan wouldn't tell me where we're going, only to wear something nice. So, I decided to wear a handkerchief-style dress that hits just below the knees. Nice and flowy in a soft white summer fabric. A little drape in the back, but not too much, just enough to do what it needs to, as Jasmine used to say.

I feel my fingers shake as I slide on a pair of gold earrings.

Why are you so nervous?

We're dressing up.

That takes things up a notch, doesn't it?

I pull out a nude lipstick, and then put it back.

Girl, do the red. If he's taking things up a notch, shouldn't you?

Glancing at myself in the mirror, I'm glad that I decided to pin my hair to the side so that it drapes nicely down my right shoulder.

The ruby red lipstick stares back at me.

Is it too much?

There's a sudden ping from my phone, so I grab it and see a text from Donovan.

`I'll be there in five minutes.`

`Okay. I'll head down.`

I grab my gold clutch and phone and then make my way toward the front door.

My phone rings again and I hit the answer button. "Okay, I'm ready, I promise. I'm walking out the door now."

"Raine? Raine, it's Vicky. Sounds like I caught you on your way somewhere."

I freeze, my heartbeat speeding up.

"Vicky," I say, hoping she can't hear the shakiness in my voice. "Yes, I was heading out."

We both pause, allowing a moment of not speaking to exist.

"How are you and Jack doing?" I finally say. It sounds forced, awkward, hanging limp in the air because neither of us seems to know how to move to the next part of the conversation.

"Jack and I are okay. We were in the Alpharetta area a couple of nights ago on our way to visit some friends, and Jack swore he saw you walking into a building with condos in it. Your hair was different, he says, but he was sure it was you. I said that surely it can't have been you, but he was adamant. So, was he right? Are you living in the Alpharetta area now?"

"I'm here for work, but I actually live in Paris now."

"How long have you been back in Georgia?"

I can't tell her I've been in town for weeks and haven't called or gone to see them. "It hasn't been long," I say with hesitation.

"I see," she says. I can hear the disappointment in her voice. "Well, Jack and I would love to see you while you're here. It's been so long. I've been calling. I thought maybe you had a new number or something. But it's so good to finally hear your voice again."

My knees tremble.

"I'm sorry," is all I can say.

"I'm not calling to scold you. You're like a daughter to us. We want to see you."

"I know."

"Raine, she's been gone five years. We miss her too, but surely—"

"I'm sorry, Vicky. I can't talk about this right now."

A tear falls down my face.

"Will you promise to call me back?"

"I'll try."

Try. That sounds glib and disingenuous.

"Please do. There's something that Jack and I would like to talk to you about."

"I'll try to call you back, but I really have to go right now."

"Okay."

"Tell Jack I said hello."

I hit the end call button quickly, and for a moment, I wanted to throw my phone across the dark hardwood floors that the kitchen floors were made to match perfectly.

But instead, I open up my text app.

> `Donovan, I'm sorry, I got a call that took a minute. Can you give me five minutes or so?`

`No problem. Want me to come up?`

`No. I'll be down in a few. I promise.`

Promise.
I hate that I couldn't use that word with Vicky.

Chapter Forty

"YOU LOOK AMAZING," DONOVAN says as I walk toward him.

"Thank you. You look nice as well. That black suit looks like it was custom-made for you. You must have an amazing tailor."

"Tony is my tailor, and yes, he is amazing. He's been tailoring my suits for years." I can see him studying my face, and I try hard to hide what I'm feeling inside.

Shame.

"Everything okay?"

"I would tell you yes, but you're a psychotherapist, so you'd know I'm lying."

He chuckles. "I see I've finally graduated from shrink." He places a finger on my cheek and our eyes say good evening to each other. "Seriously, how can I help?"

Can you call Vicky back for me? Can you explain to her and Jack why I've avoided their calls for the last five years? Can you look them in the eyes for me and tell them that I can't do the same because all I would see is the eyes of my dead best friend staring back at me?

Can you do that for me?

"I wish you could help me, but I've been running away from something that I'm afraid is no longer going to let me hide from it."

"Hey. We don't have to go out tonight, okay? How about we just stay in and just talk? I've been told that I'm a pretty good listener. We can always arrange something for another night."

I give him a soft tap on the shoulder. "You're a shrink. You're supposed to be a pretty good listener. Besides, I didn't wear this ruby red lipstick for nothing."

He leans over and kisses me lightly. "No, you sure didn't."

"Well, I feel much better now. You have that effect on me."

He kisses me again. Our eyes close as we each linger in the moment.

"Are you going to tell me where it is we're going?"

"Salsa dancing," he says, stepping back and then opening the passenger door for me.

"I've never been salsa dancing," I say excitedly as I slide in, allowing one leg to show for a moment before he closes my door.

I look up at him and see that he's blushing.

Nice payback.

"There's this great family-owned restaurant called Mary's Place that has a dance floor," he says as his skin returns to its natural color.

I try not to grin but can't help it when he wipes his forehead.

"On the first Saturday of the month, they bring in a live salsa band."

"You know, your sister gave me the impression that you were…"

"On the boring side? Staid?"

"Something like that," I say as we pull out into traffic. "But so far, we've been to listen to a band in the park do a tribute to Stevie Wonder, then we went white water rafting. On our third date, you took me to this old-time ice cream parlor and a jazz concert, and now we're going dancing."

"So, what you're really saying is that this shrink isn't boring?"

I reach over and give him a playful pinch. "Psychotherapist."

"Look at that, I've graduated again."

"Well, that depends on how well this salsa night turns out."

"Oh, I plan on it turning out great."

I raise my eyebrows.

"I don't mean it like that. Trust me, I'm an old-school kind of guy in that area, but you're not making it easy." He glances over at me, and I smile. "What I meant is that I plan on using the dance floor to keep you in my arms all night long."

"Is that right?"

"It is, but now that I think about it, I'm not sure you're going to be able to keep up with me on that dance floor," he says with a grin as we hit the expressway. "I am an excellent dancer and salsa can take some time to learn."

"Don't you worry, I'm sure I'll catch on pretty quick."

Chapter Forty-One

I ROLL THE WINDOW down as Donovan moves through traffic. The wind will probably mess up my hair, but I don't care, needing a little wind in my life right now. I close my eyes, and I remember that time Jasmine and I were heading to Orlando in my father's bright red Cadillac.

The breeze was perfect for two girls who thought the world of Disney would bring them as much joy and fun as the wind did upon our skin that day.

Man, I miss her so much. I still can't believe she's gone.

I wish she were here so I could tell her about these last couple of weeks with Donovan. She would have been so happy for me.

"What's on your mind over there?"

I open my eyes slowly. "Just thinking about a time when life seemed so much simpler."

"You sure you want to go tonight?"

I look over at him. "I'm positive, besides, I can't have you thinking I can't keep up with you on the dance floor now, can I?"

He smiles and even in the moonlight, I can see his dimple emerge, comforting to me for some reason. "How do you know how to salsa anyway?" I ask as we move off the expressway.

"Ruthie taught me."

"Why am I not surprised?"

"She was a woman of many talents. Being an exceptional receptionist and gardener was just a few of them."

"It seems we're both thinking about the ones we've lost tonight."

He reaches over and places my hand inside his, giving it a squeeze.

"I can't wait for you to see this place."

"I can't wait to see it as well. How many times have you been there?"

He glances over at me. "If you're asking if I've brought other women here—I've been here with other women."

"A lot of them?"

"If Ruthie, my sister, and my mother count as a lot, then, yes."

I laugh. "I didn't see that one coming."

"It's Ruthie's sister Mary who owns it now, but it was Mary's husband John who first opened it as a family-owned restaurant in New York, around the late sixties. He was born in New York, but I believe his father was Cuban and his mother is from Puerto Rico. John's parents blended their cooking and dancing styles, then taught everything to John."

"I bet the food his parents taught him to make was amazing."

"On the menu tonight, you'll see that one side has a few custom dishes from John's parents, and the other has some of Mary's family favorites, including items such as collard greens and the best peach cobbler you could ever experience in the South."

"Nice. So how did salsa dancing come into it?"

"Next to the restaurant in New York, there was an empty space, so ten years later, after marrying Mary, they opened up a dance studio that taught salsa, the mambo, and even tap.

"When John and Mary moved here to Georgia in the early eighties, they opened the place we're headed to. It was big enough for both a restaurant and a dance studio. After John passed away, Mary renamed the restaurant, turning the studio space into the dance area there today."

"So, they only have the dance area open on the first Saturday of the month?"

"For salsa, yes. But that's because they fill the rest of the month with the mambo, swing, and tap."

"Swing? Are you serious?"

"I am. It's a ton of fun. Briana loves it."

"This place sounds special."

He glances over at me again. "This place is very special to me. I promised Ruthie that if I found someone I thought was special, I would bring her here."

Our eyes lock for a second, the sounds of passing cars drowned out. I reach over and place my hand on his shoulder. "So, you think I'm special?"

"To be honest, when I met you at that Waffle House, I thought so."

All this time?

My heart skips a beat.

Chapter Forty-Two

I'M IN LOVE WITH this place.

This place that's full of history.

I'm in love with its vibes, its rhythm. Its uniqueness.

I love the way the sound of laughter spreads table to table as people engage in conversations, also in food that smells amazing.

I love the smiles so full of life and happiness.

In fact, a smile has completely taken over Donovan's face as he watches me take it all in.

"Welcome to Mary's Place," he says.

"It's packed," I say as a waitress rushes by, holding a tray filled with desserts that would make any mouth water.

He looks around. "It is. It's always packed. Follow me."

He grabs my hand and I follow him to a table marked "reserved."

"To me, this is the best table in the house. You can see everyone from here."

I slide into the booth and look around again.

To our right, there's a family enjoying a piece of chocolate cake. The little boy gets a little of the frosting on his nose and the mother reaches over to smear it all over his face. They each laugh and I find myself giggling and enjoying their moment.

On our left, a man and a woman sit engaged in a conversation. But what I notice even more is the look in his eyes as he listens to her talk.

Donovan reaches over the table and lays his hand on top of mine. "Look down at the table," he says. "What do you see?"

"I've never seen anything like this," I say as my fingers trace the outlines of a man and a wooden box carved into the top of the table.

He picks up a card from a metal holder. "Read this," he says, handing it to me.

I take the card from him and as I read the story of Henry Brown, a man who mailed himself to freedom using a three-by-two-foot box, and I find myself wanting to cry.

"Are all of the tables done like this?"

Donovan reaches over and wipes a tear away from my cheek. "They are. John wasn't just a great cook. He enjoyed carving the stories of history into the wood of each table. He carved a different story on the top of every table you see. It took him years to finish them all. Mary had cards made up and placed them on each one.

"People love the tables. They feel like when they come here to eat, they aren't just getting good food but going back in time, a chance to live the journey of those who made history."

"And experience something special," I say.

"Exactly. Look over there."

My eyes follow his pointed finger to a board on the wall.

"They use that board to help people remember where they last sat. That way, every time they come back, they get a different table and get to complete the journey. Once you've finished the board, you can purchase a T-shirt that says, 'I've journeyed into history.'"

"Is it just the tables in the main dining room?"

"It is. There are tables out back in the garden area, but only the ones in here were hand carved by John."

I start counting how many tables there are.

"Twenty-four," he says before I can finish. "So, if you come once a month, you would complete the journey in two years." He picks up his glass of water and takes a sip. "You want that T-shirt, don't you?"

I nod my head. "I do."

He laughs. "I'm glad you get this place. That means a lot to me."

"And to us." We both look into the eyes of someone I assume is Mary. She has the same cheekbones and comforting smile that Ruthie had. "We haven't seen you in a while, Donovan."

He stands up, but she waves a hand, telling him to remain seated. "He's such a gentleman, my Donovan. You don't find men like him anymore. My John was like him," she says, looking into my eyes to see if I'm worthy of sitting across from him.

If I'm someone special.

When a smile spreads across her face, I see Donovan's shoulders relax.

Did I just get her seal of approval?

"You have kindness in your eyes like my Donovan. Some people in this world don't; you look into their eyes and see nothing. No kindness, no compassion. They're like blank pages just walking around. Their lives will never amount to anything worth writing about because they don't *do* anything worth writing about. Things like helping people. Loving people. And being loved by people.

"Or just one." She winks at me. "In you, I see kindness and compassion, but also pain. You and Donovan also have that in common."

She slaps her hand on the table, then looks over at Donovan. "You see what I did there? I could have had your job when you decided to move on."

"But then, who would cook the amazing food that I smell?" I say.

"Oh, she's sharp."

"Mary, this is my *friend*, Raine."

"I know who she is. Raine Reynolds."

"She goes by Jamerson now," Donovan says quickly.

Was that a hint of jealousy I heard in his voice?

"My sister loved your books. I hear she even got Donovan over here to read a few of them." She pats him on the head like a mother intentionally trying to embarrass her son. He shrugs, and I can't help but laugh.

"Mary, can we order?"

She gives him the biggest grin. "I already know what you're going to have."

"What does he normally get?"

"Only my world-famous collard greens, two pieces of my spicy buttermilk fried chicken, green beans that we slow cook in my homemade seasonings, and of course, my award-winning peach cobbler."

"That all sounds so good. I think I'll have that as well."

"Don't worry about all the fat; you'll work that off when the salsa dancing gets started," she says, and then calls over a waitress who quickly takes down the order and then rushes off. "That's Misty, she's new here. Cute as a button, but I doubt she'll last more than a week. I only hired her because she's trying to pay her way through college. Poor thing. She needs one of those desk jobs."

Donovan and I smile at each other.

Mary looks from Donovan to me. "Well, let me leave you two *friends* alone. It was nice meeting you, Raine. My sister was right about you, but I'm glad I'll never have to admit that to her. She was always right. It used to make me mad as all get-out when we were growing up.

"If you promise to come back, I'll have to tell you about my John. Ruthie was the one who picked him out. Like I said—that woman was always right."

Just as I go to say something in response, Misty drops a glass on the floor.

"Child!" Mary shouts.

Donovan and I burst out in laughter.

"Poor, Misty," I say, after taking a sip of water.

"They have something stronger than water if you'd prefer a glass of wine or a beer."

"I think I'd rather hear what Mary meant when she said that Ruthie was right about me."

He picks up his own drink.

"That water isn't going to save you."

He laughs.

"But thankfully, our food will. Here it comes."

Chapter Forty-Three

MAYBE IT'S THE MUSIC.

Maybe it's the man staring into my eyes as we move to the band playing a soft melody.

Maybe it's the way his hands lie gently on the small of my back, allowing the heat of the moment to connect our skins. Even through the fabric of my dress, I feel the warmth of his fingers. *Maybe it's all of it.*

The touch, the movement, the music, but I feel good.

A kind of good that I never felt in Paris.

A kind of good that I—dare I say it—never felt with James.

A new kind of good, the kind that smells fresh like a pink peony.

The kind of good that has me wanting to ask him to be my boyfriend.

Donovan twirls me around, then brings me back into his arms.

"You weren't kidding when you said you were going to hold onto me all night, were you?" I say, just as the music moves to a faster beat.

"I wasn't, but we can sit for a minute if you like."

"I'd love to step outside for a minute and get some air."

"Sure. We can go out to the garden area."

He slips his hand inside mine as we head off the dance floor, then out to the garden area.

"I know I've worked every bit of that food off by now," I say as we find a quiet table near the lit fountain.

"Coming here is how my sister says she gets her cardio in."

"I agree. I'm sure I hit way beyond 10,000 steps tonight. And in these shoes, at that!"

He reaches down, pulls each of my feet into his lap, unbuckles my shoe straps, and then slides my feet out.

"What are you doing?"

"Getting your feet ready to hit that dance floor again."

I laugh. "You really like to dance, don't you?"

"Only when the slow songs start and only because I'm with you." He gives me a sly smile, and I'm glad the moonlight is bright enough to hide my blushing cheeks.

"Someone is putting it on thick," I say with a smirk.

"What do you mean?"

"The whole, *only when the slow songs start*, line."

"It's not a line. I don't believe in them, and I'm not ashamed to admit to wanting to be near you or wanting to spend time with you. I'll never lie to you, Raine. I may not always tell you what you want to hear, but it will always be truthful."

"I want to believe that."

"I really hope one day that you do believe that, because I mean every word."

I look up and admire the décor of the garden area. "All the lights out here and the fountain, they remind me of Paris."

"Are you missing it?"

I shrug my shoulders some, then lean back into my chair. "It's true, I do miss spending nights like this in Paris. Maybe it's me, but the stars seemed to shine so much brighter there at night. But I guess if I were there now, I'd be enjoying them without you."

He grins. "Now look who's putting it on thick."

"I'm just trying to keep up with you," I say, moving my feet and placing them on the ground. The heat of it is just what they need.

He slides his chair closer to mine. "Raine, I know it's only been our fourth date, but I would love to make you and me exclusive. Are you okay with that?"

I reach over and pull him to me so that our lips are only inches from each other. "Why do you think I wanted to come out here? It wasn't to get my feet rubbed, was it?"

"But that foot rub was nice, wasn't it?"

"It was, but a kiss would be even better."

"I can do that, too."

He places his lips on mine.

"So does that mean I can call you my girlfriend instead of my friend now?"

"Kiss me again and then I'll answer that."

"Yes, ma'am."

I hear my phone beep inside my purse.

"Looks like someone's trying to reach you."

"It's probably work."

"Hopefully, the building burned down, and they'll have to rebuild the entire thing, keeping you here for a couple of years more or longer."

I shake my head, pulling my phone out. "That sounds horrible."

He smirks. "A guy can only hope."

I open my work email. "Yep, it's from Kimberly. Last week, she emailed me to say that they weren't going to make this week's deadline due to a delay with the permits."

"That sounds true enough. Permits can take a long time."

"You don't have someone in the permit office delaying things, do you?" I ask, jokingly.

"If I did, that company wouldn't get them for a year, at least."

I laugh, glancing down to read the email.

> Hi Ms. Jamerson,
>
> Here's another update on where we are with the office in Georgia. The building management
>
> company reached out to say that they still haven't been able to get the materials needed, so construction still hasn't begun. I've enclosed pictures showing how extensive the damage was.
>
> I apologize for not sending them last week, but it appears they went into my spam folder.
>
> The delivery of the materials has been pushed to the third week in July. While they can start

> on some of the minor repairs next week (still waiting for permits as well), the majority of the repairs can't be done until the materials come in. It will take two to three weeks to complete once the materials have been received, so we're looking at mid-August before the office opens.
>
> I'll keep you posted.
>
> Best,
> Kimberly

I toss the phone on the table. "Well, it looks like they can't get the office open until mid-August."

He leans back in his chair and smiles. "I'll take it. The kids don't come back until the third week in August, and I don't have to be back until the week before. We've got the rest of June, all of July, and one week in August, so I guess my clock really starts now."

"What clock?"

"The way I see it, I've got the rest of this summer to make you fall in love with me, and then a year to make you never want to leave me."

"That's your plan, huh?"

"I'm just being truthful."

"I see."

"So, Raine Jamerson, are you ready for me to try to win that heart of yours?"

I start giggling like a schoolgirl as he leans in again for another kiss.

"I don't know. I've never had someone trying to win my heart before. Don't I need to win yours?"

"Isn't it obvious that you already have?"

Chapter Forty-Four

THANK GOODNESS THEY AREN'T busy this morning, I think, sauntering up to the counter to place my coffee order, stressed out and trying desperately to get my nerves to calm down.

I look down; my hands are shaking.

"Let me guess, a French vanilla latte."

Turning around to see who's talking to me, I see Briana standing there looking extremely tired.

"You must be working late."

"I am," she says, placing her purse on top of the counter. "I'm showing a client a condo in your building, and they could only meet me this evening. If I hadn't already had three other showings earlier today, I wouldn't mind, but girl, I'm tired. And I never get tired. My mother calls me the human version of the Energizer Bunny."

"Did you bring your gold pen?" I ask with a grin.

"My brother and his big mouth. I swear I'm going to have to remind him that I'm supposed to have brother confidentiality."

"Isn't it patient confidentiality?"

"Same difference," she says with a slight smirk. "You're here late and look stressed, what's up with you?"

"I've had a long day."

"Why? What happened?"

"I hit a dog."

She gasps. "Are you serious?"

"I wish I wasn't."

"Is it still alive?"

"I rushed her to a vet, and she is, although barely."

"I'm so sorry. How did that happen? Did you get distracted by some super cute guy crossing the street with his shirt off? Wait, you're dating my brother, so forget I asked that."

I laugh. "Thanks, I needed that."

"After something like that, I'm sure you could use a good dose of laughter and a shot of Vodka in that latte you just ordered, but I'm sure she'll be okay." Sincerity radiates from her face as my hands stop shaking and my body relaxes.

"I really hope so. I don't know what I'll do if she doesn't."

"She'll pull through."

I give her a half-hearted smile.

"Things seem to be going great with you and my brother. It's been a few months now, hasn't it?" she asks with a sudden burst of energy.

"This month, August, will make it about that, give or take a week."

"Girl, the way my brother carries on about you, anyone would think the two of you have been dating for years already. I haven't seen him this excited since he dated this girl called Joanne when he was in college."

A warning flag goes off in my head, but I try not to show it. *I'm not looking for a James redo.* "What happened to them?" I ask, casually. "He hasn't mentioned her."

"They broke up right before graduation. Personally, I was happy about it. I didn't like her, nor did my mother for that matter. She eventually married some guy who owns a couple of retail shops and properties in Atlanta.

"While I can't stand her, I would *love* to get some of his business."

"So, he's gold pen worthy, but she isn't."

"Unless she's the one writing that check."

We both enjoy a laugh as I reach out to grab my coffee. "Speaking of your brother, I hate that he has to go back to work next week." She gives me a broad smile. "What?"

"I see he's not the only one walking around looking googly eyed."

"Whatever."

"I'm glad for both of you. Anyway, when is your office finally going to open?"

"Good question. It seems like the delays keep coming. They are still waiting for certain materials, but at least they've gotten started finally."

"I'm sorry to hear that. Construction's never fun and never goes as planned. I have a client who works in an office in that building. They've been down too, of course, but she doesn't mind because now she gets to work from home."

"Considering the delays, maybe I should consider having my team do the same thing, but most of them aren't really set up for that. It's something I could look into."

"I'm sure your team isn't complaining about the situation. They're getting paid to sit at home and just wait. So, let them enjoy it. I'm sure everyone will be crazy busy once things get up and running."

"Hopefully it won't be much longer," I say as she glances over the menu. "If so, I may have to extend the lease on my place or just go month-to-month."

"Or you could just buy it."

I grin.

"I would say that you could just move in with my brother, but he's too old-fashioned for that."

"I love that about him."

"Did you just say *love*?"

"I mean..."

She reaches over and touches my arm. "Don't worry girl, your secret is safe with me."

I did use the word love, didn't I?

I smile as she looks back up at the menu.

"I've been here a thousand times and usually get the same thing, but today, I think I want something different. Let me place my order, then you can tell me all about your dog situation."

I look around. "I'll grab us a table. How long before you have to meet your client?"

She looks down at her watch. "This must be a long story. I've got about thirty minutes, but he's never on time, so let's say forty-five. I'll ask him to please text me when he's on his way."

"Great," I say, then head over to a table by the window.

Outside, people move along with their day and suddenly, it hits me that I no longer feel the world is revolving all around but leaving me behind somehow. But now, I'm one of them—the happy people, the confident ones who know where they're going, what they're doing in life.

Never did I imagine being this happy again.

Is it real? And, how long will it last?

"You look lost in thought," Briana says as she takes a seat across from me. "Still worried about the dog or something else?"

"Maybe a little bit of both."

"Which one do you want to talk about?"

She takes a sip of her coffee and we both glance out the window for a moment. She's waiting for me to begin, not wishing to push me. Eventually, she has no choice because all I do is continue looking at my hands clasped atop the table, no doubt looking miles away.

"So, what kind of dog is it?"

I appreciate the way she speaks of the dog in the present tense. "I believe she's a golden retriever, or at least, that's what she looks like to me. She's a puppy, though."

"So, tell me what happened."

"I was heading to the office so I could check on things when this dog just came out of nowhere. If I'd swerved the car to the left, I would have been going into oncoming traffic, so I had no choice but to hit her. It all happened so fast. It was awful."

"Sounds like it wasn't your fault though."

"Still, the sound I heard when my car hit her wasn't something I'll easily forget."

"Did you tell Donovan about it?"

"I haven't yet. I came here to try and calm down, but I'll let him know."

"You needed a little bit of Paris, huh?"

"I swear you should be on the stage."

"Tell you what, I'll start doing comedy if you'll start writing again."

I shrug. "You know, I'm not sure writing novels will ever be part of my life again."

"I don't believe that."

"Why not?"

"Because I've read every book you've written, and most people would kill for talent like that. No one with that kind of talent or passion for the written page quits completely.

"There's obviously something in your past that's holding you back, but once you allow yourself to leave it where it belongs, you'll allow yourself to write from the moments that fill your life now. Or you could be like my girl Mary J. Blige and use your past as the inspiration for your craft. That woman knows she can speak about pain. When she puts out an album, every woman who's ever been brokenhearted must be at home saying, 'Speak to me, Mary!'"

I start laughing so hard the table rattles. "Girl, stop!"

"You know I'm telling the truth."

I shake my head in agreement. "She's been through some things."

"Haven't we all? One day, I'll share my sad songs with you, but right now," she looks down at her phone, "I've got to go meet this client."

"Thanks for making me laugh, Briana."

She reaches over and pats my hand. "Text me about the dog later and let me know she's okay."

"I will. I'm heading back to the vet to check on her after I finish this," I say as she stands up.

"She'll be okay, Sis."

Did she just call me her sister?

I'm sure she meant that in a "raise the fist, girls have to stick together" kind of way.

Right?

Chapter Forty-Five

MY PHONE RINGS AS I pull the car out, then make my way toward the vet's office. Vicky's name shows on the screen.

Just answer it. You've stalled long enough. It's like Briana said, time to stop letting the past hold you back.

I reach down quickly and hit the answer button.

"Hi Vicky."

"I hope I didn't catch you at a bad time again?"

"Actually, I'm heading to the vet's office."

"I didn't know you had a dog. Or a cat, or—"

"It's a long story."

The extended pause tells me that she's going to ask me to come and see them.

"Well, I just wanted to call and say hello again. I miss talking with you. Not that we talked all the time when my daughter was alive, but it was never like this."

"I know. You're right."

"To us, Raine, you're still family."

"To me, as well. I'm really sorry that I still haven't called you back or come to see you and Jack. But I will."

"We understand your reasons. We really do. We represent the past and all the pain that comes with it. We get it. But Raine, there's something we really want to talk to you about."

I sigh heavily. "Okay."

"Really?"

"Yes. Jasmine would kill me if she knew how I've been acting toward you guys; frankly, I'm ashamed of it."

"We all handle loss and grief in different ways. She would understand."

"No, she'd call me out on it in a heartbeat."

Vicky laughs. "My daughter was a straight shooter, wasn't she?"

I nearly choke on her words. Years later, and I can't help but want to cry when I think about her. "Yes, she was. I loved her so much."

"She knew that. And I knew that—and it's why I'm pestering to see you!"

We laugh. She pauses speaking as she knows I'm pulling into the parking lot of the vet's office, then parking the car. "Jack and I are heading to Florida but would love to see you before we leave."

"I thought you guys didn't head that way until November."

"We're thinking about moving there actually, so we're leaving early this year, and we may stay until spring to look at a few homes while we're there."

"I'm sure Jack would love that! He enjoys golfing so much."

She laughs again. "I know. I'm afraid that if we do live there, I'll never see him."

I join her in her laughter. "Probably not."

"It's so good to talk to you like this again."

I lean back into my car seat. "I agree. Again, I'm sorry I was so distant."

"Its water under the bridge as they say. Now, how about coming for dinner next Saturday?"

"Sure."

"Thank you. Jack will be so excited. We'll see you at seven."

"Okay."

I click the end button, then undo my seatbelt. As I stare out the window and listen to all the dogs howling at the vet's office, a weight has lifted off me.

Briana would just call that the past.

Chapter Forty-Six

I GLANCE OVER AT my passenger's seat; the puppy is still knocked out from the sleeping pills the vet gave her. I am so thankful to discover that she only suffered a broken leg. She was hit so hard, flung sky high.

Poor thing.

She starts to snore, and I crack up.

My back seat is packed with dog toys, a dog bed, and dog food. The vet was pretty sure the puppy is a stray, but I plan on putting out a few flyers just in case.

"I hope you like Paris, puppy," I say as I pull into my building's parking deck, and then put the car in park. "If no one claims you, you're going back with me, whenever that actually happens. At this point, I've already had to change my one-way ticket three times," I say, rubbing her fur gently.

My phone rings as I open my car door.

"Hi, how are you doing?" Donovan asks.

"I take it you got my text about what happened to me today?"

"I did. How is the puppy? Are you still at the vet's office?"

"I just pulled into my parking deck. The puppy's on my passenger seat, still knocked out from sleeping pills, but the vet said she'll wake up soon."

"They let you bring her home?"

"She didn't have a collar or anything, but she did have severe bruises around her neck. The vet suspects that her previous owners left her tied up with no intention of coming back, and she somehow got herself free. I couldn't leave her there. She's been through so much already."

"It sounds like she has."

I wasn't sure why, but his tone was weird. "You okay, Donovan?"

"Yeah, I'm just glad you weren't hurt or anyone else. Of course, I'm glad the dog will be okay as well."

"I am, too. You want to come by tonight?"

He hesitates. "I know it's been a rough day for you, and I'm sure you want to get some sleep."

"I'm tired, but I'd like to see you."

He hesitates again. "Well…"

"If you've got something else going on, you don't have to come," I say, trying to hide my disappointment.

We've seen each other just about every day. Maybe he needs a break from me.

"I'm sorry. I'm throwing my clothes on now. I'll be there in twenty minutes."

"Okay." I end the call and lean up against my car.

Maybe he's just exhausted too. He mentioned after we left the movies yesterday that he'd be up late getting lesson plans ready.

Turning around, I glance in the window to see the puppy awake. Her big brown eyes are staring back at me as I open the door, and then I take her out of the car, careful not to touch the brace on her leg.

"I'm so sorry I hit you, sweetie, but I'm going to take good care of you now." I turn her so that she can see all the stuff in the back seat. "See all that? All for you. I don't know how I'm going to get it all upstairs, but we'll worry about that later. Let's go see your new home."

Chapter Forty-Seven

IT'S AUGUST, BUT I feel like turning the fireplace on, so I grab a large pillow, place a towel on top of it, and lay the puppy down on top of it. Her head nestles into the pillow and within minutes, she goes back to sleep.

Maybe I need some of what she took.

After getting the fire started, I go to the kitchen and grab a bottle of wine and two glasses. Donovan will be here in a few minutes, but I'm starving, so I open up the refrigerator and pull out some romaine lettuce, a green pepper, yellow onion, croutons, feta cheese, and Greek dressing. Donovan likes olives, so I pull those out too, to put on top of his salad. Just as I grab two bowls out of the cabinet, the front door opens. A few seconds later, he walks into the kitchen and puts his keys on the hook next to the pantry.

"Hey," he says.

I look over at him, seeing how red his eyes are. "I'm making us a salad," I say, feeling bad that I asked him to come over when it's obvious he's exhausted.

"Sounds good." He glances over at the wine and the two glasses.

"I think we both need that tonight."

He gives me a weary smile, and nods in agreement.

"You look tired. Do you want to go and lie down on the sofa?"

He walks over to me, pulling me to him. His arms wrap around my waist, and he holds me for a few minutes without saying a word.

"Donovan, are you okay?"

"I am now. Where's our puppy?"

I smile.

I love that he said "our" puppy.

"She woke before I took her from the car, but the minute I put her down on the pillow, she went back to sleep. Snoring too! She's in the living room by the fireplace. I thought a warm fire would help her settle in."

As I finish making the salads, Donovan walks out of the kitchen and heads toward the living room. I grab a serving tray and place the salads on it with a loaf of French bread, then grab a small plate, pour some olive oil on it, and add a couple dashes of black pepper to the oil's center.

I've learned how to cook during the months that Donovan and I have been together. In Paris, my refrigerator was always empty because I pretty much ate out every night, whereas now, I actually buy groceries so Donovan and I can cook a meal together.

"You need some help in there?" Donovan yells from the living room.

"Can you come and grab the wine and glasses for me?"

"Yes, dear."

I laugh, but I can't help but wonder, *can it really be this easy?* Donovan and I just seem to have slid gracefully into each other's lives.

We enjoy each other's company so much, and the conversations between us are always smooth and uncomplicated. We can sit and talk for hours.

No drama.

When we're not together, we're talking on the phone. There have been many nights, thus far, when neither of us went to sleep until the other couldn't keep their eyes open.

Some nights, he comes over, sits on the sofa, and reads a book while I watch a movie. Other nights, I go to his home, and we play board games.

I never even knew that I liked them so much!

Monopoly, of course, is my favorite.

Briana joins us sometimes, but she hates to play Monopoly with me because I usually end up owning most of the good real estate, then she sulks like a little girl.

As he walks back into the kitchen, I look up at him, and realize… I'm falling in love.

Stop lying to yourself! You aren't falling in love, you're already in *love!*

"She's still knocked out, but she's cute. She looks like a golden retriever."

"I thought so as well. The vet says she's not a purebred but mixed with one."

"Oh, so she's a mutt then," he says, grabbing the wine and glasses off the counter.

"If so, she's a cute mutt," I say, following him into the living room with the tray.

Donovan tosses a few pillows on the floor, and we plop down in front of the coffee table.

"You know, I just realized that we never eat in the dining room."

"Do you want to go and eat in there now?" he asks.

"Not really. That fire feels good."

He leans over and kisses me. "How are you doing?"

I sigh. "I was a mess earlier," I say, looking over at the puppy. "But now that I see how comfortable she is, I feel so much better. Briana had to remind me that it wasn't my fault."

"I'm sure that was a hard choice to make in that split second."

"You have no idea."

He looks toward the fire, a hint of sadness crossing his face.

"You're not ready to go back to work yet, are you?" I ask, thinking maybe that's it. We've enjoyed just getting together when we wanted, but starting Monday, that will change. "Did you finish getting your lesson plans ready?"

He leans over and kisses me again. "June and July went by fast, but I'm eager to see some of my students again, although I'll hate that it means we won't be together as much. As far as my lesson plans go, I stayed up until almost two o'clock working on them. Then, I got up this morning and went to the school to make sure the lecture hall that I use was on the schedule and that my office had been cleaned."

I relax. *Yep, that was it. I knew it.*

"Sounds like you had a long day."

"I did, but now I'm starving."

"Me, too," I say, handing him his salad.

"This looks good, Chef."

I smile, proud of myself, even though it's just a salad. At least it's something I didn't purchase prepackaged for a change.

"Do you want some of this bread?" I ask, breaking off a piece, then dipping it into the olive oil. He puts his fork down and looks over at me. He looks troubled.

"Raine, why didn't you call and tell me about the accident?"

I put my bread down on the side of my bowl. "What do you mean?"

"I mean, you sent me a text message, but that wasn't until much later."

"I'm sorry. I was a mess there for a while, and I just… I just needed some time to process it all." I reach over and place my hand on top of his for a moment. "You have to understand that it's been just me for the last five years. I'm still getting used to having a boyfriend."

"I can understand that."

He turns and glances over at the fire again.

"Please don't stay mad at me."

He turns his attention back to me and then moves closer. His fingers gently touch the side of my cheek as he brushes back a piece of my hair that has fallen. "I'm not mad at you. I'm in love with you. And as ridiculous as this sounds, I just want to be your everything. I want to be the one you rely on. All the time. The one you reach for. I don't know… It kind of hurts that you didn't—"

I move closer to him, wrapping my arms around his neck. "Shh. I'm sorry. I'm sorry, I'm sorry!" Tears prickle my eyes, his words so sweet and emotive, they break me. Perhaps that's why I don't—can't—share easily. Because I am scared of relying on him and then maybe, someday and for some reason, losing him. Sometimes, it's easier to rely on only myself.

Our eyes connect, the fire dancing between them.

"You don't have to say it back. The love thing. It's okay. I just wanted you to know how I feel. How much you mean to me."

I lean in, pressing my lips upon his, praying that somehow, through this kiss, he can tell how I feel about him too; I can't seem to get the words to slip from my lips.

Why?

"What are we going to name our puppy?" he asks as he gently pulls back.

I look over at her. "Let's name her Ruthie."

His eyes join mine. "I agree. She's a strong little thing. Yes, let's name her Ruthie."

Her eyes open slowly as she lifts her head and looks up at both of us.

"I guess she heard that and likes it."

Chapter Forty-Eight

"TELL ME ABOUT JOANNE," I say as Ruthie adjusts her body, so she isn't lying on her leg brace.

"My sister and my mother couldn't stand her."

I chuckle. "That much I know. Your sister told me. Girl talk."

"Why do you want to know about someone who hasn't been in my life since college?"

"You've never mentioned her. We've talked about James and me."

"I never really asked you about James. You talked about him, and I only listened."

I pick up my wine glass and take a sip. "You listened as my boyfriend or as my ex-therapist?"

"We only had one session, Raine."

"But I told you a lot during that session and since you and I have been together, I've pretty much opened the book to you about my life. I just want to be able to fill in some of the pages of your story. That's all."

He looks over at me.

"What?" I ask, trying to understand the look of annoyance on his face. "Why are you looking at me annoyed?"

"I'm not annoyed, I just want you to ask the real question about Joanne."

I place my glass on the table. "Fine."

He shifts his body and looks me directly in the eyes.

I clear my throat. "Were you in love with her, and if she were to suddenly reappear in your life, would you still have feelings for her?"

"I'm not James, Raine."

"I know that."

"Are you sure about that?"

Now, I'm annoyed. "Yes, I'm sure about that. What's that supposed to mean?"

"You're in love with me but you couldn't allow yourself to say it out of fear. Obviously, when my sister mentioned Joanne to you, it struck an uneasy chord in your mind and that's why you couldn't say it. But my relationship with her was so long ago. It's unfair to expect me to behave the same as he did. It was James who let you down, Raine. I deserve your faith in me."

Sometimes, I hate that he wasn't just a psychotherapist, but also a darn good one.

He moves close to me on the sofa, taking my hand in his. "No. If Joanne were to divorce her husband and come running to me to confess her love for me, I wouldn't have feelings for her. At least, not feelings in that way. I will always care about her, but it wouldn't be love.

"Did I love her while we were dating? Yes, I did. But she didn't break up with me. I broke up with her."

"Briana didn't tell me that," I say, almost in a whisper. "What happened?"

"We wanted different things."

"Like what?"

He sighs. "I'm going to say this and please don't get upset."

My body shifts some in anticipation.

"Joanne wanted kids, and at that time, I didn't."

"Oh."

"I know what happened to you, Raine, and I know you'd give anything to have a different situation."

I lower my head for a second. He reaches over and lifts up my chin.

"Look, I know that we aren't discussing making a more serious commitment yet, but if we do get there, I want you to know that if adoption is something that you want, I'll be okay with it."

Well, here comes the tears!

My bottom lip is quivering, my heart so ready to embrace him. "I am in love with you, Donovan," I finally say, "I'm sorry that I couldn't say it earlier. And you're right."

He leans over and places a kiss on my forehead. "I see my plan is working."

I hit him softly. "Whatever."

"Now, I just have to help you see that you never want to leave me."

I laugh. "So, your clock's still running?"

His eyes look down at my lips playfully.

"Absolutely," he says, then kisses me.

Chapter Forty-Nine

THE HOUSE LOOKS BIGGER than I remember.

I sit outside Vicky and Jack's place, telling myself repeatedly not to hit the ignition button.

Not to turn the car back on and drive as far away as I can.

I look over at Ruthie. "You ready for this?" She barks. "No, huh. Me, either. But remember, I'm depending on you to protect me. From myself. Right?"

She barks again, jumping on the spot, giddy with excitement. She's a funny little thing.

Just as I place my hand on the ignition button, Vicky opens their front door and motions for me to get out of the car. Letting out a heavy sigh, I pick up Ruthie, then open my car door.

The moment my feet hit the sidewalk, the memories of Jasmine and me playing out here in front of their home come flooding back.

Hopscotch was one of our favorites, something we played until we must have turned fifteen.

Vicky steps out onto the front porch, no doubt able to tell how much I'm struggling to take another step.

I take a deep breath and then move toward the porch steps.

My heart is heavy, huge fat tears rolling down the sides of my face one after the other, but I keep moving until I'm all the way up the steps.

Vicky reaches out and grabs me, pulling me into her as a mother would, wrapping me and Ruthie into that wonderful maternal embrace as the tears fall for us both.

"I'm so sorry," I say it over and over.

And she cries hard too, saying, "I love you. *We* love you. Thank you for coming."

"I'm so sorry though!" I cry, my tiny voice caught in so much emotion, emitting a kind of humorous squeak. Only, neither of us can laugh at it because this is raw and real and visceral.

"Stop that now. You're here, that's all Jack and I care about."

She looks down at Ruthie. "Who's this little guy with the broken leg?" she says, reaching over and taking Ruthie out of my arms.

"The little guy's a *she*, and it's a long story, but the short version is that she's mine now."

"Jasmine did say you always wanted a puppy."

Jack comes to the front door, and I go to hug him, repeating that same *sorry* over and over.

"We missed you, kid," he says as he wipes away a few of my tears.

"I missed you guys as well, I really did."

"Well, let's get inside before the neighbors start to wonder what the heck's going on over here," he says, giving Ruthie a quick scratch behind her ears before stepping aside to allow Vicky and me to enter the house.

"Her name is Ruthie," Vicky says to Jack as we walk into the family room.

The old green paint that I remember is gone, replaced with a fresh coat of cream paint. The sofa that Jasmine and I used to jump on isn't there either, replaced now with a more contemporary couch and matching chair.

The once too "busy" leaf-patterned carpet has been replaced with hardwood floors, and there are barely any photos on the walls.

"We've put it up for sale," Jack says by way of an explanation as I continue to look around.

"Jack, can you grab a pillow and a towel to lay the dog on?"

"You don't have to do that. I can put her outside on the back porch."

"Nonsense. I'm sure she'd rather be inside. She's been through such a lot, bless her. Plus, even though it's August, it's still warm out there."

"Well, that's true if you really don't mind. She'd rather be anywhere I am."

"She so cute," Vicky says as Jack returns with a pillow and a towel. And a small dog biscuit. Goodness knows where he found that; they don't have a dog, do they?

Jack eyes me looking quizzical in the direction of the bone-shaped treat. "Oh, this? It's been in the cupboard since we did a bit of dog sitting for the neighbor."

I smile and say, "I almost don't recognize this place. It's been a while."

Laying Ruthie down on the pillow, we all watch as she takes a moment to settle in, struggling to do that funny pup thing where they spin around and around before finally lying down. "There. It looks like she's settled."

"What happened to her leg?" Jack asks.

"It's a long story," Vicky says with a smirk. "But she belongs to Raine now."

Jack claps his hands together and Ruthie looks up. "Well, that's all that matters, isn't it?"

Vicky nods.

"I see the old piano in here is gone too."

"We sold that thing about three years ago," Jack says. "Now you can actually see the room." He looks over at Vicky and gives her a wink.

For as long as I can remember, Vicky had wanted to get rid of that piano, but Jack would never agree to it.

"We've upgraded just about every room," Vicky says as we walk into the kitchen.

"Wow," I say as I take in the vastness of their kitchen island. "That thing can fit at least eight people. It's beautiful."

"I almost hate to give this new kitchen up," Vicky says. "I always wanted a huge island in here."

I glance around the rest of the kitchen, stopping when I see a picture of Jasmine and me on the refrigerator. "We were about ten there," I say, taking the picture off the appliance door. "I remember complaining that day about how much I hated my curly hair. Jasmine told me to get over it because that was the hair that my mother gave me and since my mother was beautiful, so was I and my hair."

We all laugh as I place the photo back on the refrigerator.

"That was one of her favorite photos," Vicky says as she walks over to a cabinet and then pulls out a couple of wine glasses.

Jack grabs a bottle of wine, opens it, and then pours each of us a glass.

Vicky walks over to the kitchen table, Jack and I following behind like ducklings.

They begin talking about all the stupid things Jasmine and I used to do, some of which I never knew they were aware of. The conversation goes on for another thirty minutes and the laughter flowing through the air fills my heart with unexpected joy and thankfulness.

I didn't realize how much I needed this until this very moment.

"How long do you think it'll take you to sell this place?" I ask after a couple of moments of silence.

"We hope we can get it sold quickly," Jack says.

He and Vicky exchange a look, and I wonder what that's all about.

"So, what did you two want to talk to me about?" I ask, looking at Vicky.

"Why don't we have some dinner first, and then we can all sit down and talk." She looks at Jack who nods in agreement.

"Okay," I say, feeling a wave of uneasiness in the air as Vicky gets up and walks over to the stove. "You and Jack can go ahead and head to the dining room. I'll bring the food in there."

"Do you want my help?" I ask.

She smiles. "The salad and everything else are already on the table. I'm just bringing in the lasagna."

A warning goes off in my head.

Vicky always made that lasagna when she felt I needed comfort food.

Chapter Fifty

"THAT LASAGNA WAS AMAZING," I say, pushing my plate away. "It was always great, but that sauce was amazing."

"I found this new recipe and thought I'd give it a try."

"I've actually been doing some cooking myself."

Jack and Vicky both look over at me.

I laugh. "It's true. I even learned how to make egg rolls and lots of other stuff. I'm pretty good at it if I do say so myself."

"Oh!" cries Vicky. "I remember that time you and Jasmine tried to make biscuits, my whole kitchen was covered in flour."

"It took us forever to get the kitchen clean that day."

Vicky looks at Jack and he nods.

"Well, I guess we should get into things," Vicky says.

I feel my stomach tightening.

"When we were cleaning out Jasmine's apartment, we came across her journal."

"I didn't know she kept one! Never saw her as the journaling type!"

"We found it in her nightstand."

"Can I read it?"

"Well actually, we thought you might like to have it," Vicky says as Jack stands up, and then walks over to a box in the corner of the dining room. I never noticed the box sitting there.

He pulls out a black journal, a slight tremble in his hands as he walks back over, then hands it to me.

I take the journal and run my hands across the outside of it, afraid to open it and see her handwriting inside. Scared to read her thoughts.

"Wow," is all I can say.

"We felt the same way when we found it," Jack says.

They both go quiet as Jack sits back down.

"Is there something in the journal that I should know about?"

Vicky stands up this time and walks over to the buffet table. She opens up a drawer and pulls out what looks like a birth certificate.

"Well, we found this inside."

I place the journal down on the dining room table and take the birth certificate from Vicky.

"At first, we didn't know what to make of it, but after reading her journal and learning about what happened to her in New York, it all become clear."

I read the certificate, seeing Jasmine's name on it as well as the name of her son.

"She named him after you, Jack," I say, looking over at him and seeing the tears in the corners of his eyes.

"Jonathan Jack Shoemen," I say, glancing down at the certificate again.

"At first," Vicky says, "we were hurt because she never told us. But after a year went by, the hurt began to subside, and we knew we had to try to find him."

I place the certificate down. "Wait, are you trying to tell me that you found Jasmine's son?"

Jack nods.

"But she didn't want that. She told me herself."

"We know. But if you read her journal, you'll see that she began to feel differently after she told you."

My eyes move to the journal.

"Where is he?" I ask. My voice is shaking, my emotions are all over the place.

"He's seventeen years old and attending a private high school in Florida."

"That sounds expensive."

"His adoptive parents can more than afford it."

"You've met them as well?"

"We have."

"So that's why you're selling the house and moving there."

They both nod at the same time.

"How did you find him?"

"It took a few years using a private investigator. At first, his adoptive parents weren't thrilled about us seeing him."

"I'm sure."

"But the mother and I started talking regularly on the phone and she began to see that all we wanted to do was get to know him."

"How did he take it? How did you tell him who you were?"

"Thankfully, they'd never hidden from him the fact that he was adopted, so that part wasn't as hard as we thought it would be. But the hard part—"

"The hard part was not telling him why his mother gave him up for adoption," Jack says, finishing Vicky's sentence.

"How did you get around that?"

"We honored our daughter's wishes, and we lied. Funny how you spend about eighteen years teaching your child to always tell the truth. Then she teaches us how to lie."

We all laugh, raucously.

"We told him that his mother got pregnant from some guy she met one night and that she was so drunk she never even got his name."

"How did he take that?"

They look at each other again.

"Let's just say we could have thought it through better. The little scenario we concocted admittedly wasn't the best. He was hurt and angry, and didn't want to see us for a while," Jack says. He reaches over and places his hand on Vicky's, reminding me of how Donovan does that to me. A warm feeling pulls at my stomach. I miss him, yet I only just saw him.

"Things are still a little rocky, but I think we're getting there," Vicky says with a weary smile.

"I'd love to meet him one day. When you think he's ready, of course. I have to ask the obvious. Does he look like her?"

They both nod again.

"You can see Jasmine in his eyes. He's taller than she was at that age. He plays football, so he's quite strong and has that athletic build. But he's also kind, smart, and has a good sense of humor," Jack says.

"He inherited that from you, no doubt, Jack."

He smiles proudly. "As well as my striking good looks."

"He has scouts following him," Vicky says, cutting us each a piece of apple pie and then putting it on plates.

"That has to be exciting for him."

"He's a great quarterback," Jack says.

"Where is he going for college?"

"Time will tell. He may decide that he wants to play baseball. He's also a pretty good pitcher."

I take a deep breath. "Sounds talented. And sounds like he's at a really good school. My father would have loved him." I place my hand on the journal and allow it to rest there for a second before moving it away. "This is a lot to take in though."

"It is. Imagine how we felt at first."

I shake my head. "I can't. I really... Honestly, it feels impossible."

"We've learned in all of this to just take things one day at a time."

"That I can relate to, although, at times, it's not an easy thing to do."

"Why did you stop doing your novel writing?" Vicky asks abruptly, just as I go to put a piece of pie in my mouth.

I place my fork down. "I guess I lost the desire to do it any longer. Jasmine played such a key role in why I started writing in the first place."

"But you letting it go is like letting her go. She wouldn't have wanted that, and you know it."

"Jasmine wasn't the only person who played a role in my decision to start writing books. James had a lot to do with it as well. You, see?"

"Yes, I do see, but stopping what you enjoyed isn't punishing him, is it? He's dead, Raine. It's only punishing you. Writing was in you. Sure, they both encouraged it to come out, but did you write those books for them or for you?"

I stop and think hard about her question.

"I guess, in the beginning, I was writing for James, then I wrote for Jasmine when she became my publicist, but now that I think about it, in the end, I was writing for me."

"You can *still* write for you," Jacks says.

I shrug my shoulders. "I don't know. I don't know whether I want to do it or if I can. I just don't seem to have the same motivation I once had."

"Sure, you can," Vicky says confidently. "And you will."

"Everyone seems so sure about that. But I don't know."

"Everyone?"

"My real estate agent, Briana, seems to think I'll start writing again as well."

"Then she's a very smart lady," Vicky says with a hint of banter.

"She is. We've become good friends. Let me know if you guys need a real estate agent; I can introduce you to her."

They look at each other again.

"Every time you and Jack give each other that look, it makes me nervous."

Vicky gives me a reassuring smile. "We'll have to stop looking at each other, Jack."

He laughs.

"If you're talking about Briana Carter, we actually know her. It's a small world, Raine! She isn't our agent, but she introduced us to the one we're using."

"Why didn't she take the listing herself?"

"For one thing, it's not like we're around the corner, and I believe she primarily handles the Alpharetta area. We're all the way out here in Conyers. A bit far, don't you think?"

I nod in agreement. "That's true. Well, I'm sure the person she recommended is amazing as well. She's impeccable, Briana is. Nothing's too much trouble."

"She is. We've had a few people interested and we could get an offer in soon," Jack says, enthusiastically.

"That's great. I'll definitely come down to Florida to visit you guys, that I promise," I say, standing up. "Well, Ruthie and I better get going. It's over an hour's drive back, as you know, and it's already after nine."

I pick up Jasmine's journal and place it in my purse, warmed in my heart by their gesture of letting me take it. It would have been her most personal item. And they chose me to keep it. Again, the sudden urge to hug Vicky comes over me.

When I look over at her, however, there is only sadness on her face.

"I can leave it if you want."

"No, she'd want you to have it. We are quite sure about that. We copied a few pages, having them made into pictures for the wall."

I then understand the sadness on her face.

"I promise Ruthie and I will come see you in Florida."

"That's a long trip from Paris," she says. "Didn't you say that you actually live there?"

"I did, but I might be purchasing a place here. It's still too early for me to commit to, but it is a possibility. And the owner of the property where I'm staying at the moment is eager to sell."

"Jack always says that anything is possible."

"Well, I'm starting to see more truth in that lately."

Jack and Vicky stand up, and then we head into the living room so I can pick up Ruthie.

"You'll have to tell us how Ruthie's leg is healing when we talk again. I hope that will be soon. But I know you'll be busy."

"It will be. When are you guys heading for Florida?"

"It's football season and we promised Jonathan that we'd be there for the opening game. So, we hope to head out there within a week or so if an offer comes in."

"It's a beautiful home and with all the upgrades the two of you have done, I know you will get one soon." I feel so low, so tearful again.

She's searching my face. "What's wrong?" she asks.

"I guess I need time to wrap my head around the whole Jonathan situation."

"We've had a couple of years, so we get it. There have been many things we've had to wrap our heads around, but in the end, that's what you do. If you don't, you stay stuck in the past, and who has time for that? You'll get through it, sweetheart."

I reach out and hug Vicky, then Jack. "I'm so glad I came. And I'll definitely call soon."

"I'm sure you wanted to text us and cancel," Jack says with a light chuckle. "But we're so glad you didn't."

"So am I," I say, opening the front door and stepping outside. "If you guys are still here next weekend for some reason, maybe I'll bring my boyfriend with me for dinner."

"Who is this boyfriend?" Jack asks, suspiciously.

I grin. "If you know Briana, then you probably know her brother Donovan. We've been seeing each other for a few months now."

There's a slight flicker on Vicky's face as she reaches out to hug me once again.

"We'd better see you and Ruthie in Florida, young lady."

"Yes, ma'am. We'll be there."

She reaches over and gives Ruthie a pat on the head.

"Maybe Donovan can come as well, and that way, you and Jack can get to know him."

She looks up at me. "It sounds like things are getting serious between the two of you."

"I know! And it's only been three months."

"Well, love has a way of conquering all sorts of things. Just remember that."

Chapter Fifty-One

MY PHONE RINGS THE moment I put Ruthie in the passenger seat and close my car door.

"Hey, I haven't heard from you all day," Donovan says as I start the car up. "I stopped by your place and saw that Ruthie wasn't there either. Where did the two of you run off to this evening? I was beginning to think you'd absconded."

"Ha, no chance. You don't get rid of me that easily!" I turn to the dog. "Someone sounds like they were missing us, Ruthie." I give her a quick rub. "I'm sorry," I say as I pull out into the road. "I forgot to mention that I was going to have dinner with Jasmine's parents tonight. They're selling their house and moving to Florida. And get this," I continue, "They know your sister! She actually recommended a real estate agent to them since they live out in Conyers."

He doesn't say anything.

"You still there?"

"Yeah, I'm still here."

"I know it's late, but you want to come by tonight?"

"By the time you get home, it will be almost eleven. You know what they call a visit when a guy comes by a woman's house at that time of night."

I burst out laughing.

"Well, we can't have that now, can we?"

"*I* can't, but you on the other hand…"

"Whatever," I say, happy to hear a little humor in his voice. For a moment there, I was beginning to worry that something was wrong. "There's the man I love."

"I do hope so."

"Didn't you notice I had no problem saying it aloud this time?"

"I noticed. Now stop talking before I beat you to your place."

"You know—"

"Not an option," he says, before I can finish my sentence.

"You're no fun." I hit the end call button.

Chapter Fifty-Two

THE SUNDAY MORNING SUN wakes me, and as I turn over, Ruthie lifts her head.

"Good morning, girl. You ready for your walk?"

Her tail starts to wag.

I throw the covers off, automatically tapping my phone to see what time it is.

"Eight o'clock. Guess we better get a move on. Donovan will be here around ten."

Just the mention of his name sends Ruthie into a happy state of barking.

I walk over and pat her head to calm her down.

"Let me jump in the shower, then we'll go outside, okay?"

She lays her head back down. "Good girl," I say, heading into the bathroom.

I turn on the water to brush my teeth, and when I look in the mirror, the comment that Vicky made about Donovan and me pops into my head.

"Things are getting serious between you two," were her words.

Maybe not wedding dress serious yet, but yes, it's getting serious.

What am I going to do?

Can I see my life without him back in Paris?

Do I even want a life without him?

As I turn the water off, my heart is sure of the answer.

~

My phone pings as I make my way back into the bedroom.

Ruthie is sitting by my bedroom door. "Almost there, girl. One more minute, okay?"

She barks.

I hear my phone ping again, so I dash out of the bathroom and over to it.

Picking it up, there's an email from Kimberly.

> Hi Ms. Jamerson,
>
> I know it's Sunday, but the building management company emailed me to say that the office is finally ready. They wanted to know if you could come by in the morning for the inspection.
>
> I am happy to get in touch with your team today as well.
>
> Best,
> Kimberly

"Finally!" I say as I start typing a reply to her.

Ruthie begins to bark excitedly, so Donovan must have come in. "He's early, girl." I walk over and open the bedroom door, smiling because she gets as excited as I do to see him.

"Donovan, can you let Ruthie out while I finish up an email?"

"Sure," he shouts back. "Back in a few minutes then."

After sending the email, I make my way to the kitchen to get breakfast started. *Me, fixing breakfast. It's been amazing, I must say.*

Ten minutes later, Ruthie barks. *They must be back already.*

"I'm in the kitchen," I say. "Want me to scramble your eggs, or do you just want them hard boiled this morning?"

But it's not Donovan. It's Vicky entering the kitchen with Ruthie.

"Vicky?"

"Sorry, I know this is a surprise."

"It is." I walk over to hug her, but she stops me.

"I saw your boyfriend; he's the one who told me which place is yours. I hope you don't mind that I brought Ruthie back in with me?"

"Of course, I don't mind! Is everything okay? You look so serious. Where *is* Donovan?"

"I asked him not to come up."

"Why?"

"Is there somewhere you and I can sit and talk?"

"Sure. Follow me."

My hands shake as we head to the living room, Ruthie following us.

Maybe she wants the journal back.

"That view is beautiful," she says, taking a seat on the sofa. "Stunning, in fact."

I glance out the window. "It is pretty amazing," I say.

I sit in the chair across from her and Ruthie eases beside me, looking up as if she can sense something bad is about to happen, because normally, she sits by the fireplace.

"What's going on? Is Jack, okay? Did something happen with Jonathan?"

"Raine, you will find this shocking, but I'm actually here about Donovan."

My knees start to tremble, and I feel a turn in my stomach.

"What about Donovan?" My tone is defensive, but I don't mean it to be.

"Jack told me that I shouldn't come today. He told me to stay out of it, but when I asked you if things were getting serious between the two of you, the response you gave said I had to come."

"You're scaring me, Vicky. What's this all about?"

She inhales slowly.

"There's no easy way to put this, so I'm just going to say it because it's obvious that he hasn't told you."

My heart drops as the words "he hasn't told you" fall from her lips. "Told me what? What hasn't Donovan told me?"

She looks me in the eyes. "That he was the one who killed Jasmine."

I stand up and almost let out a fit of laughter in response. "That can't be true."

"I wish it weren't, but it is."

"I don't believe you!" I spit out. "No, Vicky, this isn't right. I'm sorry, but I just don't… I-I can't believe it."

"Raine, have I ever lied to you?"

I shake my head slowly.

Jasmine.

The memories of a young girl who played dolls with me and taught me how to wear high heels when we were ten comes flooding into my thoughts.

The same young girl who got her Sunday best dress covered in melted black tar when we played by the side of the road, poking at the smelly black goo with sticks in the heat of the sun.

My best friend.

The girl who held me close when my mother died and let me cry all night without saying a word.

I can't believe, no, I won't believe that the man I love is responsible for taking her away from me.

Because he's my new life. He is all I have. He is the one who lifts me up, makes me laugh, dries my tears, and grounds me. He is the man who inspires me and believes in me and pushes me to be the best version of myself. Donovan is kind and honest and up front. Not a liar. Not a man who hides from his girlfriend the fact he has inadvertently killed…

My Jasmine.

I sit back down and turn my body toward the window because I can't allow myself to look into her mother's eyes.

Vickie's voice is weak and timid. Yet she is determined.

"You and I both know that I wouldn't say such a thing if it weren't true. Maybe Jack was right. Maybe I shouldn't have come. But I did and now you're aware."

I place my hand over my heart.

Not again.

I can't feel it beating.

I lower my head into my hands and notice Ruthie staring back. “I’m so sorry, girl.” I stroke her head and she whines, feeling my anguish, nuzzling into me. “Can you tell me what happened?”

Vicky exhales. “First, let me say that it wasn’t his fault. It took me a long time to accept that fact. True as it may be, it still wasn’t easy.”

“This isn’t easy.”

Her voice softens.

“That day, a mother let her little boy’s hand go so she could send an email. The little boy had a ball that rolled into the street. He went after the ball.

“Donovan was coming down that street at the same time that the little boy dashed out. Jasmine had just opened her car door when he went swerving right to avoid hitting the little boy. His car hit Jasmine instead. She was killed instantly.”

I can’t move or speak, watching the tears fall from Vicky’s eyes.

“Was… was he charged or anything?”

“No, no. Of course, he wasn’t charged, because as tragic as it was, it was an accident. He and his sister came to see Jack and me for about a year afterward, quite often in fact, even though he could barely say a word when we got together, and it was like he was in deep shock. He even wrote us a letter asking for our forgiveness.”

She reaches inside her purse and pulls out a white envelope.

“I didn’t come over here to be mean, but I thought you had a right to know,” she says as she stands up. “Because you love him. I could hear it in the way you spoke about him.”

“I… I really don’t know how I feel about him right now.” I look away, through the window, anywhere. This is awful.

“Vicky?”

She looks down at me as I turn back towards her. "You're wondering if Jack and I forgave him?"

I nod my head.

"I know Jack has. He forgave Donovan even before he brought us the letter." She pauses as I wipe the tears that stream down my face. "I've tried. Really, I have. I keep telling myself it was a tragic accident and deep down I know that every word of that is true. But, at the same time—"

She sucks in a giant breath, readying herself for what will come next.

"My daughter is gone." She takes a seat again. We're both lost in memories, allowing the silence that looms in the air to take over. "You know," she finally says, "I just realized something."

"What's that?" I ask in a whisper.

"If Donovan had made a different decision and hit that little boy, that mother would have lost a son. A little boy who had his whole life ahead of him. I don't believe Jasmine would have wanted that." Her body sinks into the sofa as she leans back. "You know the mother never even took the time to come and see Jack and me. Yet, Donovan did." Vicky looks over at me. "I guess I'm really angry at her, not Donovan." She stands up again and lets out a sigh. "Jack was right, I shouldn't have come." She walks over to me and reaches for my hand, pulling me out of the chair. Her finger touches my cheek, catching a tear that falls. "All this time I've been directing my anger at the wrong person, and now here I am trying to force you to be angry with him as well. It wasn't fair or right. I'm so sorry. You've been through so much."

I don't know how I'm supposed to respond, so I stand here, body trembling. Emotions all over the place.

"I meant what I said yesterday, Raine, that love conquers all. Even this," she says. "I'll let myself out and tell Donovan that he can come up. I'm sure he's waiting downstairs. Forgive him, Raine. I just did."

She moves forward slightly, hugs my stiffened body, and kisses the top of my head. But it's as if she isn't really there. My thoughts won't free me to take in anything else that is going on around me. I can't even begin to unravel what I'm feeling.

All I can think about is… he's said nothing to me this entire time.

Nothing.

"I don't want to see him. Can you tell him that?"

She nods, and I watch as she walks out of the living room, heading for the front door.

Every part of me wants to scream.

Chapter Fifty-Three

I LOOK DOWN AT the white envelope resting on my lap. Ruthie sits up and starts to wag her tail. My shoulders tense up; Ruthie's actions mean that Donovan is headed in my direction. And of course, there he is. He says not a word, just running his hands through his hair, pushing back in the actions of an anguished man who doesn't know what he can say to rectify this.

Our eyes meet. In his, there is only pain and perhaps a hint of fear.

Maybe he's afraid of losing me.

In my eyes, hurt and a sense of betrayal lurk.

Can I forgive him? Can I do what Vicky asked of me?

Our eyes are looking for answers that our lips are not able to provide.

He moves to the sofa and his eyes drop to the white envelope on my lap. Ruthie doesn't move. She stays at my side just looking, head tilting, ears pricked.

Maybe she feels his betrayal as strongly as I do.

We both sit there staring at nothing, thinking about everything.

He places the key to my place on the coffee table, offering it back unquestioningly, even if I haven't made up my mind on anything yet. There hasn't been time.

I look down at it, then back up at him.

"I know I should have told you. I was going to do so today. That's why I came early."

My lips don't move to respond. *What do you think I can say to that?*

"When I walked into that coffee shop and saw you, all I saw was another chance. I wanted that chance, wanted the opportunity we'd missed over twenty years ago."

He pauses for a moment and looks out the window.

The sky is clear. The sun is shining. But for us, it's storming. *So,* I think. *It's one of those days again, a day in which the world carries on as if everything's fine, when mine is broken.*

"I knew that James already had a girlfriend," he says. "He'd mentioned it during the conversation on our way to the Waffle House, that they were having issues and were on the verge of breaking up. Why, I don't know. We didn't even really know each other well enough—in my opinion—to have a conversation like that. But I guess he felt like he could talk to me after I told him the field that I was in. He wanted to know what he should do.

"He felt that you represented the new direction in which he wanted to take his life. For him, one path was with a woman he wasn't sure he wanted to be with anymore, the other path was with you.

"He made a choice. I knew you deserved better. But that day, you made a choice as well. You chose him. My point in telling you this is that we all make decisions that put us on a path. Some decisions we make are good and some aren't. But whether good or bad, our decisions lead us down a road in life. So, that day, when I was driving," he says calmly, "I had to make a decision, a fast decision in a split second, maybe the same as you when the dog ran out in front of your car. How is my decision different or worse?"

"Because with me, it was a dog I hit," I spit out, but I know he is absolutely correct. Everyone would save the child in that situation, wouldn't they? So, I am not angry about that.

Even Jasmine would have said to save the child!

I am angry at the lack of openness.

And honestly.

He should've told me.

"I made a decision to save a child, Raine," he pleads. "Tell me, how can that be construed as wrong?"

He looks down at the envelope in my lap again. "You'll see in that letter that all I had was a matter of seconds to make that decision. A decision that would change my life forever.

"A decision that would change a woman's life just leaving work that day. A woman who was the best friend of someone. The daughter of a mother. The love of a father."

"I didn't even see Jasmine there until it was too late."

He looks over at Ruthie.

"I know you, Raine. I know you would have made the same choice. Ruthie is proof of that."

He stands up.

"Look, I don't know what you want me to say. I don't want to lose you and saying that I love you right now won't mean much, but I'm putting it out there and asking you to remember that you love me too. I'm asking you to give us a chance, and that you forgive me."

He moves toward the hallway.

I could be watching him walk out of my life. But I do nothing to stop it.

Ruthie sits up, but she also doesn't follow.

Chapter Fifty-Four

HOURS HAVE PASSED, BUT I still can't seem to make myself move.

My legs feel the same as my heart does right now.

Numb.

Ruthie starts licking my hand, hungry. I almost call out to Donovan to feed her, catching myself.

I watch Ruthie walk out of the living room. I know she's heading for the kitchen, so I place the envelope on the coffee table and tell myself not to look at that wretched thing lying there too.

The key to my place.

A part of me wants to pick it up, to hurl it at something. But the other part of me wants the person to whom it belongs.

Now, Ruthie is growing agitated in the kitchen, knocking her bowl up against the wall, so I quickly look back at it.

Why though?

Why didn't he tell me?

Ruthie starts to bark. "All right, girl, I'm coming," I shout at her.

In the kitchen, I pull her food out of the cabinet, my eyes lingering on the words engraved on the outside of her bowl.

Our puppy.

"I guess it's a good thing that you can't understand everything," I say, watching her eat. "If you could understand, if you could understand what's really going on, would you tell me to forgive Donovan?"

She stops eating for a second and barks.

"Was that a yes or a no?"

There isn't even enough wine in the bottle that sits next to the key to help me get the clarity that I so desperately need right now.

I breathe deeply, open the envelope, and then pull the letter out.

> Dear Mr. and Mrs. Shoemen,
>
> Words can't express the depth of
> how sorry I am for your loss.
>
> I know my sorrow for what happened will
> never be as deep as your own, nor even
> a tiny fraction of it. But I wish I could
> have made a different choice that would
> have saved them both that day, and I
> hope this may provide even the smallest
> measure of comfort for both of you.

> You see, I've spent the last year playing through what happened, as I know you do too, lying awake at night...trying to figure out if there was something else, I could have done.
>
> There wasn't.
>
> I didn't see your daughter until it was too late. She wasn't there, and then she was.
>
> Even though it was a catastrophic accident, I am writing to ask you both to please forgive me.
>
> Sincerely, and in deepest sympathy,
> Donovan Carter.

I fold the letter back up, returning it to the envelope.

I'm having a hard time forgiving that he didn't tell me, that he did the one thing he swore he wouldn't. He lied to me.

James lied to me.

Donavan knows what I've been through and how much pain lying has caused me. Would he ever have told me?

If so, when?

Chapter Fifty-Five

FOR THREE AND A half months now, I've approached each day at work with one goal in mind.

That goal is to get back to Paris. But today, all I want to do is bury my head in my pillow.

Even Ruthie is quiet this morning, missing him, I'm sure.

I accidentally slipped and said Donovan's name last night, and it sent her into a barking fit, taking at least thirty minutes to get her to calm down.

As for how I am feeling, who can say?

No. That's a lie.

My heart still hurts.

And yes, I miss him.

Terribly.

The key he left on the coffee table is still there, the letter sitting next to it. I've reread it a thousand times, hoping that one day, after reading it, I'll achieve what Vicky and Jack did.

To forgive him.

The sun is rising now, the birds are awake and tuneful. "How about I stay home today so you can go play at the dog park this morning?"

She barks as I grab my phone, and then open up my work email to send an out of office message to my team.

"There. I'm all yours today, Ruthie," I say, tossing my phone on the nightstand, and then moving to the side of the bed. "I think I'm going to need coffee first, girl."

She follows me to the kitchen.

I pour her a bowl of food and then make myself a cup of coffee. It's nothing like the fresh coffee from the little shop around the corner, but it has worked for me for the last few months.

Ruthie stops eating and looks up.

"What's wrong girl? You don't want any more?"

She starts barking, then skitters out of the kitchen, her tiny claws *tap-tapping* on the wood floor as she scurries toward the front door. The doorbell rings just as she makes it there.

Through the peephole, Briana stares back at me.

"Go away, Briana."

"Raine, open the door. I'm not here for Donovan or for me. I'm here because of Mary."

I open the door. "Why? What happened to Mary?"

"The funeral is this weekend. I've tried calling you, tried texting you, but I knew you would want to be there. She was a fan of yours."

"And I am one of hers."

"Can I come in?"

I move aside.

Ruthie runs between us and starts to lick her hand.

"She's gotten so big. Her leg looks like it's completely healed."

"She's been doing good with it," I say as we head to the living room.

She takes a seat in the chair and Ruthie plops down on the floor beside me as I sit on the sofa.

We both look at the key and the letter.

"Give it a chance, Raine. Forgive him."

"What do you want me to say to that?"

"The truth."

"What do you and your brother know about the truth?"

"Raine, I know you're hurting but don't take it out on me. For the record, I told my brother to tell you what happened the moment I became aware that Jasmine was your friend."

"Correction. She was my *best* friend. My lifelong friend. Like a sister."

"I'm sorry."

I lower my eyes. She didn't mean anything by it, but I can't help but be salty.

"Are you going to come to Mary's funeral on Saturday?"

"Is Donovan going to be there?" Ruthie stands up quickly and starts to bark.

Why did you say his name?

"I see she still loves him," she dares to say.

"I don't think she ever stopped, but dogs are so much more forgiving, aren't they? Dogs don't see all the nuances."

"No, but dogs know when they find a good person! It's instinctive, Raine. And my brother is a good person, a very kind person! Very loving—and he loves you! It's unfair to both of you!"

"Oh, it's unfair, is it?"

She leans forward in the chair.

"Raine, let's stop this. You and I are friends. More than that and you know it."

What I know is that I'm pouting like a child, and I can't seem to stop myself.

"Yes," I finally say, "I will be there for Mary."

She pulls out a piece of paper and lays it on the table next to the letter.

I know she did that intentionally.

"Then here's the address to the funeral home. It starts at two. The repast will be at the restaurant," she says as she stands up.

Ruthie walks over to her, and Briana bends over to pat her on the head. "I'm not going to tell *him* that you're coming, before you ask."

"How is he?"

"He's the same as you, only worse."

"Well, I haven't gotten one message or call from him."

"He knows that the only way it's going to work between you two is if you decide to…"

"Forgive him?"

"More like, love him enough to forgive him. To choose a future with him over the past."

"That's a lot to ask when we only dated for three months."

"And yet, in three months, you both fell in love. Any fool can see that, sense that. Some people live their whole lives and never taste or touch what you have."

"I never thought I could love so hard after James, but then I met…" I look down at Ruthie. "Him. He made it so easy. He fit in my life like that perfect pair of blue jeans."

She smiles. "Girl, you know I like to shop, but I'm still looking for those myself."

We both laugh.

She walks over and hugs me. “I’ve missed you too, Sis,” she whispers in my ear.

“Bye, Briana. See you Saturday.”

Chapter Fifty-Six

MY EYES SHIFT FROM one black dress to another.

"Maybe, I shouldn't go, huh, girl?"

Ruthie looks up at me and barks.

"Yeah, you're right, Mary was a friend. I'm going."

I pick up one of the dresses, slipping it on.

"How do I look, Ruthie?"

She barks once more and wags her tail.

"Thank you, I was hoping you liked this one."

In the mirror, I see a woman with her natural curly hair standing right in front of it. *And thank goodness you threw out all that pink a few weeks ago.*

"I'm going to see him today, girl. Going to see your dad. Not that I want to. Or maybe I do."

She walks over and licks my hand.

"You know what? I'll tell him. I'll tell him that *you* miss him. That you can't eat or sleep, and he needs to get himself over here for a visit."

She follows me out of the bedroom and into the living room.

I pick up the key and hold it in my hand for a few seconds before placing it back on the table.

"I don't know if we're ready for that yet, girl."

She takes her paw and scrapes the key onto the floor.

I pick it up, putting it back on the table again.

She barks.

"I'm not sure if I'm ready for that yet, girl."

She barks once more.

"Okay. Okay." I pick the key back up and put it in my purse, then look down at her. "I'm not making any promises here."

She wags her tail.

The doorbell rings and she sets off barking.

"That must be your sitter, Ruthie. Let's go let her in."

Ruthie runs to the front door, barking uncontrollably. "You're in a funny mood today. You must know that she's taking you to the dog park today," I say as I finally catch up to her. I pat her on the head a few times to try to settle her.

To no avail. Now, she's pawing at the door. "What's gotten into you, Ruthie? Let me get the door open."

She shuffles backwards to make room for me to open up the door.

So, I tug it open without even looking through the peephole... and freeze. "Donovan?"

"Hello," he says, Ruthie smothering him with her kisses.

"What are you doing here?" I say after Ruthie finally calms down.

"Mary passed away. The funeral's today, and I just couldn't go without coming here first. She made me promise."

He looks over at me. "Sorry, I know that was a mouthful."

"I know Mary passed away. Why do you think I'm wearing this black dress? Briana came by and told me a couple of days ago."

"Of course, she did."

We stare at each other, both trying to hide the nervousness that we each feel.

Ruthie barks and we both look down at her.

"She's so happy to see you," I say.

"She's gotten so big."

"She has. The vet says she's going to get even bigger."

"I always wanted a big dog."

I try to hide my smile, but it's hard when he looks so good. *And smells like fresh pine combs.*

"You look great by the way. I like your hair like that."

Don't blush, girl. You're wearing a black dress.

"Can I come in?"

"Sorry," I say, moving aside to let him in. "I only opened up because I thought you were Ruthie's sitter."

He glances at his watch. "I'm sure she'll be here in a few minutes."

"Who says it's a *she*?"

He smiles, and my heart already wants to hand him that key.

"I had this whole speech prepared," he says as I stand there holding my breath. "But now, all I can get out is, 'please say that you forgive me,' because I can't do this any longer, Raine. These three months have been more than I can bear."

He takes a few steps closer to me, but I say nothing.

"I'm in love with you. Please, say that you forgive me." He stands so close, my lungs soak up his cologne, and his breath tickles my neck.

"Please say that you forgive me," he whispers.

Too many tears fall.

"Don't! Don't come this close to me!" I cry. "You know how much you have hurt me! It's not all about you and what you want, you know that?"

"You're trembling," he says as he gently pulls me to him, kissing my neck.

Then my cheek. "And yes, I know that," he whispers, stroking my hair. "It's about *us.*"

Then our lips touch, me passing my tears across to him as they drown my face.

"I missed you so much," he says, as I cling to him. "I've missed you every second of every day. Do you know that? I need you to know that."

He pulls back, and our eyes connect as if they've never been apart.

I lay my head on his shoulder.

"Raine, I need to hear it."

I look back up at him. "Yes, I forgive you. Yes, I miss you. And yes, I'm in love with you."

He leans in to kiss me again as I wrap my arms around him and allow the tips of my toes to rise to meet his eager kisses.

The doorbell rings.

We both grin.

Ruthie begins wagging her tail.

"I need to let the sitter in," I say, pulling back slightly.

One minute. He pulls me back to him and then kisses me. "I love Mary, but now all I want to do is stay here with you."

Ruthie barks again.

"And with you, too, Ruthie," he says, and then moves aside so I can open the door.

As I let the sitter in, something stirs inside me. It isn't hurt this time.

It's happiness.

"I gave the sitter a bigger tip for staying longer for us," Donovan says as I watch him walk back into the living room. He sinks down to the floor where I am, then pulls me into his arms so that my back rests against his chest.

"I'm glad we went."

"Me too. I'm really going to miss her."

"What's going to happen to the restaurant now?"

"My mother will take over as the General Manager."

"You look like your father," I say. "Briana, on the other hand, is like a younger clone of your mother. Although your mother doesn't look her age at all."

"Everyone says that. No one believes me when I say that she's sixty-eight."

"I can't believe your parents have been married for fifty-two years."

"My dad always jokes that she raised him. He was eighteen when they met, and a senior in high school. Can you believe, he hit her with a football! By accident, he claims, but who knows? It got her attention anyway. He says he fell in love with her when she picked up the football and threw it back at him. Hard. *At* him, not to him!

"They were married six months later. She was sixteen. She had me a year later."

"I can't imagine being married at sixteen, let alone starting a family at seventeen."

"Things were different back then. But the nature of love hasn't changed."

"What do you mean?" I ask.

"My father knew my mother was the one for him. Some people think it takes years to fall in love with someone, but I believe that when you find the one who fits, the one who *completes* you, why wait for time?"

Am I hearing him right, is he about to ask me to marry him?

Will I say yes if he does?

"The other day, I told your sister that you fit me like a perfect pair of blue jeans," I confess.

He laughs. "I guess, for me, you would be like my suits, then."

I nod my head with a grin. "They do fit you perfectly. I think the one you had tonight was a better fit than any others. Did you wear that one on purpose?"

"Did it work?"

"Absolutely not. Hideous!"

I turn my head, and we kiss.

"Man, I love you, Raine." He pauses. "I think you know that I want to marry you. But I'm not going to ask you until I think you're ready."

"You don't think I'm ready now?" I turn and face him.

"I think you forgave me, but no, you're not ready to choose me yet."

"How do you know that?"

"I'm a shrink, remember?"

"You teach now though," I say, with a playful smile. "You lost the entitlement to be called that word."

We hear Ruthie snore, and we start laughing.

"She's sleeping peacefully. She always does when we have the fire going," I say, turning around so that we're back in the same position as before.

Donovan places his chin on my shoulder. "I wasn't sure if I would ever hold you again," he says softly. "It broke me."

I wrap his arms around me so that he's holding me tighter. "Did you ever see that movie, Jerry Maguire?" I ask.

"Sure. Why?"

"Something you said earlier reminded me of it."

"What did I say?"

"It was about how a person completes you. There's a scene toward the end, the one where he finally realizes that he had the biggest moment in his life and his wife wasn't there to share it with, so he rushes to the house and there's this woman's divorce group there and he just starts rambling because he's trying to convince her to not give up on them.

"She doesn't say anything because she's shocked that he's there. And so, he says to her, 'You complete me,' and she then tells him, 'Shut up, you had me at hello.' The moment I saw you tonight, the moment you said hello, that's how I felt."

"So, you're basically saying I did all that rambling for nothing? My prepared speech?"

"It was more like begging," I say, jokingly.

He kisses me on the neck. "When it comes to you, I don't mind begging."

"Someone is pouring it on thick," I say.

"I'm just trying to keep up with you."

With that, he places his hand on top of mine. "When you're ready, I'm going to put a ring on that finger."

Chapter Fifty-Seven

THEY SAY SPRINGTIME IS a good time to shake the dust and winter cobwebs off things. As I place my hand on the stainless-steel door handle, I feel like I'm removing the cobwebs and revealing something that has been hidden within my corners.

The smell of coffee fills my lungs as I step inside. A sense of comfort fills my entire body.

"Welcome to Books and Coffee," a young lady with bright orange hair says as the door closes behind me. "Let me know if you need help finding anything."

"Thank you. Where is your women's fiction section?" I ask.

"Third aisle on the right."

I move down the aisle slowly, looking for books by authors with the last name Reynolds. Knowing that it's more than possible that I won't find one of mine.

It's been too long, girl.

I stop and take a deep breath.

Oh, my goodness.

It's buried on the bottom shelf, but staring back at me.

The last book I wrote.

There's a red discount sticker on the front, but I don't care because it means that my presence in the literary world didn't fade away completely, as I had feared it would.

I'll have to tell Briana she was right. She said that I would find one here.

I pick the book up and then knock the dust off with my hand.

Don't cry.

A tear falls.

Who cries in a bookstore?

I turn it over, open the back flap, and stare at the photo of myself.

Hello, old friend.

I missed you.

Not that I miss being Raine Reynolds, but I do miss what the book itself represented.

Me, as an author.

Me, doing the one thing that I could say I was passionate about.

The young lady with orange hair comes down the aisle.

"I see you found your own book."

I stare at her. "How did you know it was me?"

"You did a book signing here years ago. I was eight at the time, but I remember you. I'm more of a sci-fi reader myself, but my mother and my sisters all love your books. I recognized you the moment you came in."

"It's been a long time," I say, looking down at the book again.

"More than five years ago, give or take is when that one came out. Are you going to start writing again?"

"I think I've got a story or two still in me."

She nods her head. "That's cool. I own this store now, so if you start doing book signings again, would you consider my shop?"

"I'll let my publisher know, if I still have one."

"I'm sure they would be happy to have you back again."

"I hope so."

"I guess you won't know until you call them."

I look at her and smile.

Young but wise.

"You're right. I guess I need to make that call."

"You can use my office if you want. I'm a firm believer in doing things when the moment is moving me to act. It's how I bought this bookstore."

"Really? You made that decision in a moment?"

"I did."

"You'll have to tell me that story."

"Nice pun. But it's not that long of a story. One day, I came in here to buy a book and the owner tells me that he's selling it. I immediately asked him how much. He jokingly tells me to make him an offer. I think at first, all he saw was the red hair; it was red at the time, so he didn't think I was serious. But I put a number out there. It took a few rounds of negotiations, but we finally settled on something we both could live with."

"How did you have the money to buy a bookstore? Sorry, that's none of my business. It's just that you're so young."

"My dad is loaded, and he was more than happy to back me since that meant that I was finally going to commit to something. But you know what, I always knew I would own a bookstore. My father thought it was hard for me to commit, but it was just hard for me to commit to doing something that I only *liked*. I wanted something that I was passionate about.

"Are you passionate about writing?"

I let her question roll around inside my head for a second.

"I am."

"Then, go make the call. Why wait? My office is just around the corner. Next to the restrooms."

She watches as I move in that direction.

Chapter Fifty-Eight

THE SUNDAY SUN OUTLINES the corners of my closed curtains as I sit up in my bed.

Ruthie, of course, lifts her head up when she sees me move.

"Give me five minutes, girl."

She lays her head back down as I pick my phone up and dial a familiar number.

Vicky picks up almost immediately.

"Good morning," she says. "I was going to call you today. I saw your text last night. Congrats on your book deal. That didn't take long, I see."

"It was the longest two weeks of my life," I say.

"I'm sure."

I look over at Ruthie.

"I'm sorry to call you so early in the morning."

"Please. You know Jack and I are like most old people; we wake up before the sun most days."

That one gets a chuckle out of me.

"What's on your mind?" she asks.

"I could be just calling to say hello."

"Not at eight in the morning."

"How is Jack?"

"You know how Jack is. He's been in heaven, as they say, since we moved here."

"I'm sure. And how are things with Jonathan going?"

"Things have been great. He's going to the University of Florida. He wants to play baseball."

"Nice."

"So now that we've got all the small talk out of the way, what's up?"

"You sound like your daughter."

"Of course, my apple fell from my tree and onto that girl the moment she was born."

I inhale.

"I want to ask you something."

"Is it about marrying Donovan?"

My hands begin to shake. "It is."

"When did he ask?"

"He hasn't yet, but…"

"You're considering asking him?"

I grin at the idea. "I know that's weird. I know all of this is weird."

She laughs. "You're not the first woman to ask a man to marry her. I beat you to that punch many moons ago."

We both stay silent for a moment.

"I really want you and Jack to be okay with it."

She sighs. "Raine, Jack is okay with it. Trust me. And I'm okay with it."

"So, you two would come to the wedding?"

"That depends on if it's going to be in Paris or Georgia," she says with a little banter. "I'm kidding. Of course, we will come to wherever you two decide to get married."

"Are you sure?"

"Stop that. I speak for me and Jack, who's on the golf course right now. We are happy for you and Donovan. I promise."

I exhale.

"Thank you, Vicky."

"So, when are you going to ask him?"

"Tomorrow, I think."

"Why wait until tomorrow? Do it today. It's obvious it's been on your mind all night."

"It has. I think I slept for about four hours if that."

"I'm sure that was mostly because of your being worried about what Jack and I would say."

"You know me well."

"Well, I'd tell you to go back to sleep, but it sounds like you've got a proposal to plan."

My heart leaps with excitement. "I guess I do."

"Text me later and tell me how it goes. I already know he'll say yes."

"Really?"

"Sure. I saw it on his face that day I came to your place."

"I wasn't sure we'd get here."

"I knew when I left, you two would get there. Like I said that day, love conquers everything."

"I guess you were right."

"Too bad I still can't get Jack to realize that fact."

Chapter Fifty-Nine

THE DOORBELL RINGS AS I rush into the kitchen to grab Ruthie's leash.

She starts barking excitedly, then runs to the front door.

"You ready, girl?"

She barks again as I open the door.

"Hey," Briana says.

"Thanks for agreeing to watch her tonight," I say, handling her Ruthie's leash.

"You nervous?"

"I should be, but I'm not."

"I knew one day, we'd be sisters."

"He hasn't said yes, yet."

"Girl please. You've had my brother's heart since that day we were all up on the roof. Why do you think he acted like such a child that day?"

I smile, remembering that day. "We did get off to a bit of a rocky start, didn't we?"

"When two people can weather the storm before they are even married, that tells me that you two can handle whatever comes later."

I smile in agreement. "I do love him."

She reaches over and hugs me. "He loves you too," she whispers in my ear.

I grin.

"So, when is your next show?"

Her fact lights up. "I can't believe I'm booked for the next three months."

"I told you that you should do comedy. Now look at you."

"It's crazy."

"So, am I going to be the last person to use your gold pen?"

"Not yet. I think I'll have at least two more times to use that pen before I leave the world of real estate behind," she says, giving Ruthie's head a rub.

"Thanks for getting me such a great deal on this place. I can't believe I close on it next week. Do you think *he* suspects anything?" I ask, without saying Donovan's name so we don't send Ruthie into a barking frenzy.

"He doesn't."

"Perfect."

"What time is he coming over tonight?"

I look down at my watch. "He should be here in twenty minutes."

"I guess that means that Ruthie and I need to get going," she says as she puts Ruthie's leash on her. I watch as they make their way to the elevator before closing the door.

I light the last candle on the dining room table as Donovan makes his way down the hallway.

"I'm in the dining room," I shout.

"So, this is what this room looks like," he says as he walks in, and then leans up against the wall. "You look amazing tonight. I'm not sure I've seen you in blue jeans before. Did you wear those for me?"

"Are they working?"

He walks over and pulls me into his arms.

"Absolutely."

He leans over to kiss me and it's perfect, the kind of kiss that makes me say in my head, *this is it. This is what love is made of.*

This is what love looks like.

And feels like.

And yes, there was a part of me that wanted to move my hips to his rhythm like we did when we were salsa dancing at Mary's Place, but more importantly, every part of me wanted one thing…

To marry this man.

And it's not about forty years.

Or forever, for that matter.

It's just about loving him with every part of me, from the tips of my toes to every hair on my head.

"Donovan, I need to tell you something," I say, forcing myself to pull back slightly.

He looks down into my eyes and I see love staring back at me.

"Okay," he says, slowly.

"You know that in a few months, I'm supposed to go back to Paris."

A nervous look comes across his face.

"Raine."

"Let me finish," I say, trying to keep a serious look on my own.

It's hard because what I want to say feels as though it wants to burst out of my chest.

He takes a step back and inhales.

It takes everything in me not to smile.

"I had this whole speech prepared for tonight," I say softly, allowing the anticipation of my words to float in the air so we can each breathe it in and remember every second. "But now, all I can say is that I love you. In fact, I'm in love with you, and I'm ready.

"I'm ready to choose you, Donovan Carter.

"Marry me."

He grins, and then pulls me back to him, wrapping his arms around my waist in a way that tells me they've always belonged there.

"Of course," he says. "But know that you had me at 'I love you.'"

Epilogue

THERE COMES A MOMENT in life when you're standing at a fork in the road. On your left, you see the life you once had. On your right, you're staring at the life awaiting you.

It's June 8, 2019, and I know which road I'm on, knew it the moment I awoke this morning and said hello to the summer sun.

I knew it the moment I put on this wedding dress that fits me like a perfect pair of blue jeans.

I knew it the moment I slipped on these heels of which Jasmine would be proud because they're at least five inches high.

I knew it the moment the flowers arrived, Briana bringing in my veil with tears in her eyes.

In another hour, I'll be standing next to the love of my life, with Vicky, Jack, and Jonathan in the front row. Then, I'll be glad to have chosen a path that allows Donovan and me to walk down the road of life together.

In the past, it was natural to assume that Paris had saved me. But, in truth, it wasn't until I came back to the red clay roads of Georgia that I really found myself.

But in the end, it wasn't Paris or Georgia, although both had roles to play.

In fact, if someone were to look at me today, they wouldn't just see a woman in a pretty wedding dress. If they looked close enough, they'd see what really saved me.

And they'd call it love.

Book Club Discussion Guide:

1. Raine goes through immense grief and loss throughout the story. How does the author depict her emotional journey, and did you find her reactions and decisions realistic?
2. The book explores themes of infidelity and betrayal. How do Raine's revelations about James and Jasmine's knowledge of his affair affect the dynamics of their relationships? Were you surprised by any of the characters' choices?
3. Detective Tracy Thompson plays a significant role in the story, sharing her own traumatic experience. How does her presence impact Raine's healing process, and what do you think of the therapist recommendation?
4. Raine's decision to give up her writing career and pursue a new life in advertising is a major turning point. What do you think motivated this change, and how does it affect her character development?
5. The introduction of Donovan Carter as a therapist and later as a love interest adds a layer of complexity to the story. How did you feel about the romantic subplot between Raine and Donovan?
6. Jasmine's tragic death is a significant event in the story. How does it affect Raine's journey and her relationships with other characters, including Donovan?
7. The discovery that Donovan was involved in the accident that killed Jasmine is a shocking revelation. How did you react to this twist, and did it change your perception of Donovan as a character?

8. Forgiveness is a central theme in the book, with both Vicky and Raine grappling with the idea. How does each character approach forgiveness, and what are the consequences of their choices?
9. Raine's decision to propose to Donovan is a pivotal moment. How does this reflect her growth as a character, and what does it signify about her future?
10. The story concludes with Raine and Donovan planning to marry and build a life together. What are your thoughts on the book's ending? Were you satisfied with the resolution of the various plotlines?

Feel free to use these questions to spark discussions and explore different aspects of the book with your book club members.

Printed in the USA
CPSIA information can be obtained
at www.ICGtesting.com
CBHW070516220524
8854CB00004B/8

9 781732 488083